Cheeky,

Bloody

Articles

Tales for Well-Dressed Cynics
and Optimistic Ragamuffins

Cheeky,

Bloody

Articles

Cathleen Davies

4 Horsemen
Publications, Inc.

4 Horsemen Publications, Inc.
1497 Main St. Suite 169
Dunedin, FL 34698
4horsemenpublications.com
info@4horsemenpublications.com

Cover by 4 Horsemen Publications, Inc.
Typesetting by Autumn Skye
Edited by Jen Paquette

Library of Congress Control Number: 2022936708

Paperback ISBN-13: 978-1-64450-609-7
Audiobook ISBN-13: 978-1-64450-608-0
Ebook ISBN-13: 978-1-64450-610-3

Dedication

To Nephew Max, a storyteller,

And Nephew Noah, a rascal.

Acknowledgements:

Thank you to the 4Horseman team for seeing the potential in my stories and for allowing me to keep everything as English as possible.

Thank you to my mum and dad for putting up with me since birth. Thank you to all my friends who have bought the book, read the stories, helped me edit, workshopped with me, and eased my mad imposter syndrome; there are too many of you to name and I love you all, but especially Thomas, Emma, and Rati who've dealt with my nonsense the most consistently and for the longest.

Versions of some of these stories have appeared in: Another North; Severine; Muswell Press's *Queer Life, Queer Love*; Storgy; Dostoyevsky Wannabes' *Love Bites*; Miracle Monocle; Time to Tell; Please See Me; and The Maine Review. I want to thank these publishers for giving me the opportunity to share my work during the early stages.

Thank you to UEA and the University of Birmingham for helping me feel like a proper writer, even when I wasn't one.

Thank you most of all to Fliss the cat.

Contents

Three Stitches

It'd been a pleasant funeral, if such a thing existed. There were no raucous outbursts of weeping, no children asking inappropriate questions, and no mourners draping their bodies over caskets. It was the right time for Nanny to let go of life. The soil would have a better use for her than the staff at St George's hospice, where she'd spent the remainder of her days, moaning about the food, refusing to cooperate with medication, and pretending it was a disappointment whenever my mother came to see her.

"Oh, it's you," she'd say, with undisguised scorn. My mother was the only one who ever visited her, and for the life of me I couldn't understand why she kept doing it.

In my grandmother's penultimate resting place, the fuzzy, brown carpet clashed with the smell of antiseptic and the clutter of walking aids. Nanny either genuinely couldn't remember who

I was, or else didn't want to. My mother thought it was because of my tattoos.

"You could have at least covered your arms," she'd muttered through the rolled-down window when I pulled up in the carpark. It was the first time I'd seen my mother in years. I wondered how, before speaking, I could manage to do something wrong.

We'd waited with Nanny all day. We held her hand, whispered words of encouragement, asked her if she was comfortable enough. She didn't really make a lot of noise, only whimpered and complained of the cold. Any time we added extra blankets to her deathbed, she immediately threw them off and proclaimed we were trying to suffocate her. Eventually, we just stopped trying. A carer conceded that we weren't really helping, that it might be best to leave her to rest since her death could come tonight, tomorrow, or three months from now. I hoped she wouldn't die too soon. That way, I could show my face at the home the next morning, then make a speedy escape in the afternoon.

I wasn't to be so lucky. By the time we'd arrived back at my mother's house, the phone was already ringing with the news. She'd passed away. It was time to make arrangements.

I was sleeping on the sofa. My mother had downsized after I left home, exchanging the two-up-two-down for a bungalow in one of those odd little cul-de-sacs intended for OAPs. She'd kept all the old furniture, and it looked madly cluttered in such a small space. The coffee table, whose sharp corner had once gouged the scar by my left eye, was still planted in front of the sofa so that she could rest her tired feet. After that accident, I was given three stitches. The scar was ugly enough to still embarrass me. I was lucky though; it could have been worse. Any farther to the right and I would have gone blind in one eye. I pushed the table farther away from the sofa, insisting on getting it as far away from me as possible. In the morning, my mother went spare because I might've scratched the hardwood flooring.

After the funeral, we sat on the bench opposite my grandparents' gravestones. My mother lit a cigarette. My grandfather's grave was thick with weeds, but my grandmother's plot was freshly turned, which seemed strange next to all the mossy and overgrown tombs, as though even nature knew that she had lingered on earth for too long. The wake was at a small pub on the corner. Soon, we'd have to go and shake hands with the relatives I couldn't stand while cramming cold egg sandwiches into our mouths to prevent further conversation.

"It's a shame, you know," my mother said, exhaling smoke. "You never met your granddad. Now, he was a *lovely* man."

"Only the good die young," I said sarcastically, but my mother nodded sincerely in response.

"Your gran would always say, *you wait 'til your father gets home. He'll give you what for.* Then my dad would come home, all covered in paint, and he'd be too happy to see me to do anything. He'd sit down and I'd crawl on his lap, and he'd tell me not to do it again, giving me a little kiss on the forehead. Well, you can imagine my mum was fuming! She'd give me what for herself then." My mother laughed. "Oh, you kids don't know you're born. Back in our days, you were hit with belts, smacked with rulers, your ears were twisted... Can't get away with that now."

When I was nine years old, I'd spilled orange juice on a white carpet, and in response, my mother had hit me so hard that I panicked and ran away from her while she slapped at the back of my legs. I tripped and hit the side of the coffee table, causing the deep gash that needed three stitches and became a reminder of my near-miss with blindness. My mother's response to the streaming of blood had been to carry on shouting.

"I was *just* telling you to be more careful!"

On my return from the hospital, I had to scrub out not only the juice, but the blood stains that had dribbled a trail to the front door. I remembered wondering why she insisted on having white carpet through the living room. It seemed as though she'd deliberately decorated in such a way as to cause maximum potential damage so she could experience the thrill of hitting me. I wondered also if this was why she filled cups all the way up to the brim before asking me to carry them to my aunts and uncles. Coffee in one hand, tea in the other, I'd watch the liquid splash about, walking as though I was on a tightrope and feeling her eyes drill into my head. I always spilled. To this day, I'll only fill cups three-quarters full.

"People still abuse children," I said dryly.

"That's not what I meant, just that it was *normal* then, you know?" My mum shook her head. "God. No tears. A whole funeral and no tears. Isn't that the saddest thing you've ever heard?" She offered me a cigarette.

"No thanks. I've quit," I told her.

"Since when?"

I shrugged. I could've given an exact date since it was when I found out for certain, but I thought it was better to be vague.

"Maybe a few weeks."

"Ha!" my mum said. "Well, be careful to watch what you're eating. People gain weight when they quit smoking, and you've already got to be careful in that area."

I stayed quiet.

"Haven't you?"

"Yes, Mum."

The birds were twittering in a major key, sardonically. It wasn't a sunny day. The clouds hid the sky, and the trees stood crooked and naked against the backdrop, but I suppose birds had to stick around to mock the mourners at funerals.

"I mean, I tried to cry," my mother said. "When I had to make my speech, I thought, I'll clench my eyes shut and the tears will flow, but nothing. Then I looked about and thought, what am I worried for? No one else cared about this old bat. It didn't matter that her death wasn't making me sad." She shook her head. "But it *is* sad, isn't it? That it's a relief to your loved ones when you're finally dead. God, I hope that never happens to me."

I snorted. My mother looked at me with eyes like daggers.

"What the hell is that supposed to mean?"

"Nothing," I said.

"Is this seriously what you're going to do? On the day of my mother's funeral, you're going to torment me? Try to make it clear how much of a terrible mother you think I was? Well, I'm sorry, but you weren't exactly the easiest daughter. Years it took to potty train you. I was still changing sheets when you were well into your teens. Horrible." She sniffed. We were quiet for a little while.

"Mum," I asked, trying to feign genuine curiosity. "Do you remember how I got this scar just next to my eye here? I was wondering about it the other day."

"No idea," she said. "Probably one of your old *sports* injuries."

That was an old resentment I'd forgotten. My mother hated the fact I played tag football and refused to let me out of the car whenever I was wearing my kit because she said, *"A girl in a sports jersey is the mating call of the lesbian."*

"It was from your coffee table," I said, trying to keep my voice calm. "Do you remember now?"

"Oh, yes!" she said. "We had to drive you all the way to hospital. God, you cried the whole time. You were always running about like mad; it was impossible. I knew you'd hurt yourself one of those days."

We stayed quiet for a while. It was starting to spit with rain, but we ignored it. As much as I hated being here, the thought of the pub was even worse. Great aunties, great uncles. Halitosis. Waist grabs.

"Come on then," my mum said. "You can buy me a drink."

"Sure," I said. I'd get one myself, as well. There was no point in holding off anymore; I'd made my decision. I'd call the clinic on the way home and book an appointment.

We stumbled along the pebble path between the rows of gravestones. The pebbles got caught in my mum's heels, and she had to keep stopping to shake them out. Walking on the grass was, of course, unthinkable. The rain had started to come down heavily now, and it was miserable.

Across the expanse of graves, we saw a family burying one of their loved ones. Who it was I couldn't be sure because there seemed to be people from every generation: children, parents, geriatrics. They were all wearing ridiculous costumes: tie-dye t-shirts and big wigs with purple curls. Someone was banging on bongo drums, and they all sang together. They ignored the rain and, while it was clear they had been crying, all were making an effort to smile. It was strange to watch.

"What on earth are they doing?" my mother asked.

"I think these days people don't wear black so much. They want their funerals to be a happy celebration," I said.

"Oh God," my mother scowled. "How tacky."

Rat Maze

It was an old manor house set back against the hilltops, hidden by the expansive gate and bushes. Thanks to an army of horticulturalists, the garden was well-maintained. It was the kind of place that should, perhaps, have been open to the public, where families might have picnicked on the grounds or gazed in awe at the beautiful four posters, but it wasn't used for those purposes and never had been. The remote-controlled gates were camera-fitted and built solidly at fifteen-feet high.

Occasionally, period dramas liked to film there, and Rebecca would watch the crews from her bedroom. She'd sit on her bay window-ledge, the curtains drawn behind her, audaciously hoping she was ruining their shot. It always felt ridiculous. Those actors in period costumes with crinolines and orange wigs would smoke cigarettes and eat cheese and pickle sandwiches during breaks, speaking in ghastly, and no doubt affected, cockney accents. This injection of the real world into an historical setting seemed odd, but then Rebecca didn't know much about the real world.

The house was supposedly her childhood home, but normally she wouldn't be there. Rebecca lived at school most of the time. In their dorms, there were six girls to a room, the drawers beneath them barely large enough to contain all their weekend clothes, but Rebecca liked it there. It was cosy.

The virus had been exciting at first. Rebecca had joked about zombie apocalypses. She saw the younger students licking their palms and rubbing them onto their friends' faces, heard screaming in response in that overly giddy way that only little girls can achieve. A lot of people were happy to be sent home. An extended holiday, cancelled exams—what was not to like? Rebecca and her five bunkmates had cried together on the last night, but she could tell it was mostly insincere.

"I'm just going to miss you so much, like, I don't know what I'm gonna do without you girls," Sofia said, dabbing her eyes with the back of her hand, careful not to smudge her eyeliner even though they were all locked in for the night.

"It's only a month," Rebecca said, stroking her hand with her thumb, "less than, even. They'll probably call us all back next week. *Sorry, everyone. False alarm. Turns out it's just the flu.*'"

"Well, no, it's definitely going to be at least two months before the government says they'll review

10

the situation," Chardonnay mumbled in between biting her nails. Not for the first time, Rebecca found herself annoyed at Char's inability to read the room. Scholarship kids were always the most useless at conflict management.

"I'm just trying to stay positive, that's all. I mean, the world won't stop forever, will it? Over a few little sniffles? Try not to be so dramatic, Chardonnay."

In hindsight, Rebecca wondered if she'd been trying to console herself more than Sofia, although she didn't remember feeling scared. In fact, she recalled a vague flicker of excitement at the thought of sitting at home all day. She was craving a lie-in in her double bed with multiple pillows (the height of luxury compared to the matchbox she was used to). She wouldn't have to play tennis in the rain during their designated sports hour. No lights-out. No homework.

A year later, Rebecca couldn't believe she'd ever wanted this. She found out, crushingly and all at once, that she didn't know who her parents were and that she didn't recognise her home. Worse still, she learned that absence doesn't always make the heart grow fonder, and those friends of hers who'd sobbed together holding hands were easily inclined to forget her when they were no longer forced into the same vicinity.

Her house was too large for noise. The sound of a spoon clattering on the floor three rooms away was enough to make her jump in agitated shock. At first, her mother had insisted on mealtimes together. They sat at triangular points on a table far too large for their nuclear set-up. Her father would sit at the head, pretending to be in charge of the situation, while her mother donned a stoically unfaltering grin.

"Well, this is nice, isn't it?" she'd said on their first night. "All of us together. No company. No distractions. How long has it been? Gosh...' Rebecca's mother had a habit of asking questions without waiting for an answer. "It must have been when Becca was a little girl. What do you think, Charles?"

Her father, meanwhile, didn't hold much interest in the family that had interrupted his golden years.

"Perhaps," he responded, in his slow, whispery voice.

There was a shiver of desperation behind her mother's shit-eating grin, a slight panic that Rebecca hadn't noticed before. Prior to the pandemic, her mother was always in a state of relaxed busyness, constantly attending high-stake events (but events where one was expected to drink copious amounts of gin). Rebecca wondered if she was missing her lovers. They'd had to send the staff home during the crisis. Even the hedges were left alone now.

Thankfully, family meals didn't last long. They went on for perhaps a week before Rebecca's mother got sick of cooking. Afterwards, all nourishment was done in a grab-what-you-can-when-you-can fashion. Rebecca ate many handfuls of dry cereal and finger-sized portions of cheese.

There's only so much sleep one can get before becoming an over-wired jittering wreck, and Rebecca soon found that the novelty of timeless days wore away. All of her personal effects were still mostly at school. She'd packed too many clothes with her. She should've known that she might only need a few pairs of pyjamas, but no. With misguided optimism, she'd packed hundreds of outfits appropriate for various formalities and found there was no place to wear any of them. Sometimes in frustration, Rebecca would slip on a glittering frock just to wander around the house. She would shave off all her body hair and paint her face in full regalia. The corridors and rooms of the place seemed endless, and she explored them in her well-dressed attire, picking at peeling wallpaper and wiping the dust off surface-tops with her palms. Having packed so many useless things, Rebecca was finding that the objects she relied on daily had been left behind. The pack of cards she liked to shuffle as she concentrated, the scented candle that helped her sleep (the one that Sofia always blew out for her when she was already dreaming): these were all still trapped in the girls' dorms. She ached for them terribly.

The news worsened. The moments of fantasy that Rebecca considered sacrosanct and untouchable withered and died before her. Her GCSEs were no longer. Her school email was filled to the brim with cancellations and reschedulings. The kicker came when the Year Eleven prom was cancelled. The prom had been Rebecca's daydream since starting secondary school. She'd had her dress hanging in a dustcover since the beginning of Year Ten. It was an Alyce Paris in a rich, rose taupe with intricate silver beading. It flowed from her waist with netting that was just subtle enough to be classy while just extravagant enough to be glamorous. It was two sizes too small for her, but she'd promised she'd starve for it. Needs must. When the email came through to say that, unfortunately, the show must *not* go on, she screamed. It might have curdled blood had any blood been around to hear it.

Rebecca wanted to make a scene, but there was no one to perform for. She threw around the dusty tomes of children's encyclopaedias and fairy tales that had been bought (but never read) for her as a child. They thudded loudly, if somewhat pathetically, on the lilac carpeting. The weeping lasted for a few hours before Rebecca found herself with the faintest of smiles surprisingly tautening her cheeks. She supposed that a cathartic breakdown had been needed.

Thanks to a lack of proper nutrition, Rebecca could finally fit into her prom dress. She stood in the full-length mirror, tracing her fingers over the visible collarbones peeking out above the swooping neckline. Her hair desperately needed doing. She hadn't stepped in a salon in months and her delicate honey-blonde hair had slipped

down her head into an incidental ombre. Her eyebrows needed waxing too, but she looked beautiful. Even with her eyes puffy and her cheeks red
from the crying, Rebecca could still see that she
was beautiful.

Rebecca didn't take off her Alyce dress for
some time after that. It started as days and then
went into weeks, and before she knew it, the idea
of removing it at all seemed unthinkable. She
liked the way it swished around her as she turned
corners on her various walks to nowhere. She felt
far, far too small without it, and after showers,
she'd rush back into it, often neglecting under-
wear. After a while, showers didn't feel necessary
when she'd just put on the same clothes, the same
makeup anyway. It was easy to justify these odd-
ities. Who knew when she'd have the opportunity
to wear it again? If national lockdown wasn't a
time to be indulgent, when else would be?

So often Rebecca had planned her sixteenth
year with delighted anticipation, forewarned
as she was that those were sure to be the best
years of her life. There would have been parties,
dancing, boys, sexual experimentation that went
beyond the lesbian histrionics of her dorm-room.
But none of it was happening. It brought Rebecca
to a state of near abject despair. She would find
empty rooms with high ceilings to sob in so
that the acoustics added gravitas to her distress.
She rested like a princess with her elbow on the
window ledges, but the film crews had all dis-
persed, and she didn't interfere with any camera

15

angle. The grass was now full of piss-coloured dandelions.

Eventually, Rebecca decided that, although she was painfully alone, there was no reason she couldn't do her best to make her adolescence as close to the fantasy as possible.

"What? Are you serious? He said that about me?" she'd murmur to no one, gasping in pleasure at their supposed response. "Well, he's only human," she'd laugh, flicking back the few strands of hair that had become loosened from her elaborate up-do and were now dreadlocked together.

Sometimes in her afternoons gliding down the empty hallways, stopping to look in the mirror to ensure she still existed, she'd find herself slammed aggressively against a wall.

"What are you doing here? Don't you know if they catch you, they'll kill you?" she'd say, sliding her own hand up her thigh to the naked crotch beneath her dress. "Oh stop, Fredric. You know I can't deny you anything."

In these ways she amused herself, inventing friendships and relationships with those who showered her with attention, devotion, and adoration, far more than those in reality ever had. On the rare occasion she found herself interrupted by someone from this realm of existence, she'd manage to avoid them by declaring, "Dress fitting! I was just trying it!" to her baffled and uninterested parents; a father increasingly confused by the ludicrous state of the world to concern himself with the quirks of female, teenage behaviour and a mother with a creeping concern about the dwindling contents of her wine cellar.

Rebecca missed her scented candle and her deck of cards. Rebecca missed company. But there was a certain glee that she managed to cling onto in the realm of her solitude. Interactions with real human beings became something of an exhausting chore when she could be flattered and adored by ghosts, confiding in those who thought her charming and perfect, correct in everything she did. Envisioning the alterable holograph of Fredric (who she saw as an amalgamation of all those she had previously loved) excited her beyond all sense. In her bedroom, they writhed between bedsheets as she pressed her pillow against her, and in drawing rooms, she flung herself into furniture to clumsily accept his pawing, desperate kisses. Her friends, although appropriately jealous, were supportive. The great thing about imaginary friends was that you never had to feign any interest in their lives. You were very much the centre of their universe.

But all relationships require a certain drama to keep the spark alive. Soon the long, winding corridors and spiral staircases with various, empty (and sometimes frustratingly locked) rooms started to bother her. Rebecca felt like a rat pacing as she did, often doubling back on herself and retracing her steps. The sense that people were watching her grew. Sometimes she would shout: *"I know that you're listening!"* into the empty air.

Once, Fredric caught her and this embarrassed her. She hated the idea of him seeing her imperfect and vulnerable. But if anyone would embrace her madness, it would be Fredric. When her mascara and eyeliner started to crust, he would scrape it from the corner of her eyes with a gentle thumbnail.

"My darling," he'd say. "Don't upset yourself."

Rebecca knew she had to get them away from this prison. She stared out over the green flatland that contained them. She didn't know how to get out of the gate, but there was woodland where they could hide while they thought up a plan. She needed to know people weren't looking for them. They needed to create a distraction.

It was Fredric that came up with their quick solution.

"What was the scent of that candle you miss so terribly?" he asked her.

"Pine," she said, wistfully, running her fingers between each other in pretence of holding hands.

"Pine?" he asked. "Pine like this furniture? These floorboards? Or oak like the rafters in the pantry? Are you sure it isn't cedar?"

"All I know," Rebecca said, "is that when it burns, it smells like an enchanted forest."

"Well then, my love," Freddie replied, kissing her just below her ear, "let's make it burn."

With old-fashioned houses like hers, the structural integrity tended to be relatively weak. Rebecca danced with Fredric, their arms clasped together in a waltz as the crackling surrounded them. The ceiling fell through while the music in her head seemed loud enough to be audible to anyone who might pass by, and she sang, barely noticing the flames that licked the hem of her beloved dress. The smoke made her cough, but she liked it just the same. There was something Edwardian in the tuberculosis soundscape. Rebecca vaguely wondered if her parents had made it out alive.

"Oh Fredric," she said, her head resting on his shoulder. "You've made me so very, very happy."

It took a long time for the firefighters to reach them. They had a little trouble getting through the gate.

Love in the Time of Welly Vodka

I want to tell the story about the two boys I saw at a Pigeon Detectives concert, stacked together like a totem pole, arms spread wide while the audience milled under them like clumsy, bumbling ants. It was a crazy, hectic, coked-up-wearing-sunglasses-inside kind of crowd. One friend had pointed to another and gestured him to climb aboard. *Fast, fast, fast, fast, loud, loud, loud, loud.* The tiny, sweaty room had painted-black walls, and the floor was still tainted with the traces of poorly mopped-up vomit. The stink of that illegal vodka never left the premises. I don't believe it ever will.

The band were as mad as the crowd were, all curls and leather, emptying water bottles over their faces, spitting it back out at the crowd where it hung in the air like mist for a few nanoseconds before settling on us like dew. The totem pole slipped over a lot, and the top boy would splay on the floor. The supporting lad would stretch his arm down to retrieve him from the crowd, then he'd crouch down like a kid playing leapfrog to let him straddle his shoulders, making sure they made the most of the 130-second song. It was a good song. The band were playing "I Found Out' and half the crowd were only there that night in the hopes of hearing *that one song,* so the current of the pit crashed forwards and backwards, up and down, but no one in that moment minded claustrophobia. The brothers must have fallen over about five times, but they stood up and reconvened even when I could see blood trickling down from a split lip, something that might only look like the result of a brisk wind but would undoubtedly swell up huge by the morning. The top stayed on the shoulders, arms punching out sporadically, out of rhythm as he tried to balance of the top of the bottom's jumping, precarious dancing.

We sang together out of tune, chanting like a football crowd, arms reaching forwards towards the stage in a desperate demonstration of attention-seeking energy:

"Going out with! Yes, you're going out with!"

And then the screams and claps and cheers.

"Thanks for that," said the top to the bottom after being let down.

"Nah, you're alright, mate. You're alright," said the bottom to the top. The band were still basking in praise and glory, handing back the

21

phones they'd nicked, engaging in the banter that I always felt sure was planned in advance because I'm cynical about all effortless social engagement. The top looked back to the bottom, and he said, in a voice like a child on his first day of school, that same innocence and endearingness, a question neglected by most adults to avoid the inevitability of awkwardness:

"What's your name?"

And I knew then that they weren't brothers, and I knew then that they weren't friends, but I also knew that for those two minutes and ten seconds they had been. In crowds like that, you rub against skin and taste peoples' sweat more than you do when you're fucking, but it's platonic and beautiful and ugly and sexual and meaningful in ways that extend beyond the body, and the bruises and the split lips never seem to hurt and instead they become trophies like love-bites or skinned knees.

Time's Up

He lit a cigarette and tried to work out how much of the pint he had left. At first, he guessed maybe three quarters, but that was wrong. It was exactly four fifths. He'd worked that out mathematically. See, the empty part of his glass (still coated white with foam) was around two fingers deep if he held his hand sideways. All he had to do then was put the index finger from his left hand on the place where his right-hand fingers ended, and then move the right hand underneath the left index and work his way down strategically all the way to the bottom of the glass. A pint was, in total, five two-finger measurements deep, or ten fingers, he supposed. Since the top two-finger segment was empty, he had four fifths left. That made sense. He was impressed at how clever he'd been working that out. Still, he'd have to be careful. He only had five bob left and she'd want a drink too, when she got there. She'd probably be there soon.

His leg was jittering and shaking the table. He could control that if he wanted to. Normally, he stopped shaking as soon as he noticed himself doing it, but this time he just watched his lifted heel forcing the leg's erratic judder. The motion was hypnotic. It was mad that without any effort on his part, his own leg was behaving so outrageously, buzzing underneath him. He only stopped when his knee smashed against the bottom of the table. It hurt. The knee was a real sore spot. He could have spilled his pint.

It made sense that he'd hurt himself. He probably deserved it, all things considered. If she'd have been there when she was meant to have been, she'd have punched him on the thigh well before he noticed the shaking. She'd say something like, "Can you bloody sit still?" and he'd pretend he was in agony, clutch at his leg like she'd broken it. He only half pretended. She hit hard. He liked her punches though, reckoned it was a sign of affection, just like kissing, except that the punches left evidence in the knuckle-shaped bruises all over his arms and legs. It was a source of pride to have those imprints on him, and he worried when they'd started to fade.

He'd rung her up that morning to sort it out, but her mum told him she was dead asleep. He tried to convince her to wake her up, practically grovelled actually, insisting that it was a matter of grave significance, but her mum wasn't having it. Her daughter needed to rest for her A Levels, apparently. It was all bitterly disappointing.

He'd wanted to hear her sleepy voice, the way it sounded when she'd just woken up. It was deeper, sexier than normal, even though she only ever asked the time in a real vague and confused way. Course, he was just in awe that he'd managed to get her sleeping next to him in the first place. It was always on a mate's sofa with no real privacy, but he could still feel that dip in her side-body when he ran his hand over her curves, still gasped when he felt the bristles underneath her skirt. He wanted to be on a sofa with her now. He wanted to be *anywhere* with her now, but she wasn't here yet, and she hadn't come to the phone so that was that. He'd had to leave a message with her mum, who swore blind she'd pass it on, but he wasn't sure. Bit unreliable, messages, when he thought about it. He lit his next cigarette from the dimp of his last one, glanced at the clock advertising the Burton ales he couldn't afford. Thirty-eight minutes so far. Another drag.

The problem with fags was that he always wanted one, even when his throat was sore, and he could've done without. He craved them just for the way they looked, the way he felt holding one in his hand. It was something to do, smoking. He made a real effort not to look over at the clock again. It was right above the bar where the barmaid was standing, and he didn't want to keep turning round and staring, making it obvious that he was desperate for someone to show up. Instead, he looked out the window thinking about what he'd say when she got here. He'd pretend it was no bother. Say he'd just been dwelling on the passage of time. He drank some more, measured the pint again. Little more than three fifths now, give or take; he stubbed out his cigarette, looked at the clock. Forty-two minutes. That meant it took four minutes to smoke a cigarette. What could he do with this information? Start counting his cigarettes, maybe? No point. It would only cause more stress.

There was a phone box across the street. He knew her number off by heart, memorised it on the first night he met her: seven, eight, five, seven, six, nine. She'd written it on the back of his hand, and he'd spent half the night nervously going over it with biro, making sure it didn't fade away in the clammy atmosphere. She spent a lot of time dancing, jerking side to side, but she didn't spend much time looking in his direction, and he was worried that he might have mucked it up, said something wrong or acted weird. At the end of the night, she turned around, stood on her tiptoes, and snogged him. He was too nervous to kiss her back, just stood there, stiff and confused while it happened *to* him. In response, she'd shrugged, said "in a bit then," and left. It took him a full two minutes to realise he should offer to walk her back, and he had to peg it down the street to find her. She flicked her fag away but didn't say anything when she noticed him. He had to get his breath back before he could say anything either, and then he had nothing to say, so they walked in silence. It was kind of comforting, in a way. She'd kissed him again when they got to her house, and this time he managed to kiss back. He repeated her number back to her, and she'd nodded to say it was right. The muscle memory in his hand forced him to scribble her number over everything for the next few weeks. It was all over his Yellow Pages and the pad next to the telly. Seven, eight, five, seven, six, nine.

He needed to call her, but he had this premonition of leaving his seat and his drink, and the barmaid tidying it away, or someone else coming in and deciding the window booth was fair game. There'd be no recovering from that then. He couldn't even fight with them in case they realised he wasn't eighteen and shouldn't be in the pub anyway. If he got kicked out, he'd have to keep waiting for her in the cold, and it really was cold. Freezing, actually.

Or even worse, the second he left his seat to walk over to the exit would be the second she walked in. She could come in from the other door, look around, shrug, and leave, and all the while he'd be over at the phone box trying to get through to her. Not worth it. He opened his pack of cigarettes. Fourteen left. He thought he'd had more than that.

His leg was starting to shake again. It was harder to stop it this time. He shoved his heel flat against the floor and managed to keep himself still, but then he noticed that his hands were going, tapping on the table, rubbing up and down his thighs. By the time he'd stopped that, his legs were off again. It was like some stupid skit off the telly, some unfunny comedian with tinned laughter in the background. He felt all disconnected, his joints all thin and knobbly, his limbs stretching out farther than he expected them to.

His mouth was dry. It was really bothering him. He took a huge gulp of his beer, realised what he'd done, measured the pint again. One and a half fifths left. Concerning. He put a cigarette in his mouth, took it back out, put it in the packet. Checked the clock again. Nearly an hour now. They'd be closing soon.

He wanted that cigarette. His throat was dry. His throat was dry, and he wanted the rest of the pint so that he'd feel comfortable enough to have the cigarette. He tapped his hands on his lap, realised that a bruise was forming on his knee because it hurt. Downed the rest of his pint, lit the cigarette. There was still maybe a mouthful left in the glass, a mouthful because he couldn't be bothered with fingers anymore. With the cigarette he felt calmer. Underneath the table his leg was shaking but he didn't care. For the next four minutes, he felt alright. Smoked his cigarette. Finished the mouthful. His leg jittered up and down.

The move would be unconscious. He'd put on his jacket and slide out from the table, then rush over to the exit, power-walk across the road.

Get there, breathless, heart beating fast, hardly any money. The phone call would be worth it, way more worth it than another mild, another hour sat around with shaking limbs and steady fingers measuring out pint glasses and cigarettes. Dial her number. He'd be able to see her if she went in the pub from either entrance, as long as he kept straining his neck to check both sides. He'd try and stop his breathing from sounding so heavy before she picked up.

He couldn't wait to hear her voice, almost hoped she'd be asleep and that he'd wake her up just so he could hear her voice crack, the sultry moan. Fingers would drum the glass of the phone box. The phone would ring and ring, until he'd hear her say: "Hello? What time is it?" still half asleep, and he wondered if he'd buckle, and he reckoned that he would, that he'd feel his stomach drop and his legs go to jelly beneath him.

He sat in the booth. Ten to three. The pub was closing soon. His glass was empty. Nothing to lose. He looked over at his jacket, thought about putting it on. The phone box was across the road. He knew her number off by heart: seven, eight, five, seven, six, nine. His heart was beating. His breathing was quick. His legs weren't behaving. They weren't moving to stand. He sat there paralysed. The clock was ticking.

White Butterflies

He wasn't the first man I'd ever loved, but he was the first man I'd ever loved who then went on to kill himself, and I suppose that gives him a particular significance in the grand scheme of my life. I remember sitting outside with his mother while she handed over all the things from his will. This was during the part of the grieving process where I drank myself to near-death just trying to get through the weeks. A white butterfly landed on the wooden table of that bright, British beer-garden. His mother told me, her eyes wet and shining like goldfish, that whenever she saw a white butterfly, she liked to think it was her son saying hello, promising he was still watching over her. I've never been able to prevent cynicism from twisting my crooked, facial features. For this, naturally, I detest myself.

In an attempt to improve my future prospects, and also to ease my way into an early cirrhosis of the liver, I moved to mainland Europe where the wine is cheaper, and there was no one there who loved me enough to worry about that fact. Through sheer will-power and psychological repression, I forgot everything about my life from *before* and assumed that this, right now, was *it*. There was no past. There was no dead lover, no abandoned tombstone, and if I couldn't gain approval from these new, fashionable Europeans, and if I couldn't force this updated, troubled boy to shower me with adoration, then life was worthless. My failure would confirm that I was entirely unlovable and destined to die alone. So, I cried and pined pathetically, giving my heart to anyone who was cold and attractive enough that I thought they might be able to fix it, as though to fix a heart required broad shoulders and good cheekbones. I thought that by seeking approval through caring too much and being too kind, I was demonstrating that I was a good, empathetic person, but I've since learned compassion isn't really compassion if you only ever direct it towards the people you want to fuck.

At home, a sea away, a two-hour flight and a three-hour train, a friend of mine was suffering. This wasn't a friend I'd ever tried to impress. He knew me back when I had braces and poorly dyed hair, when we made cringey Youtube videos and spent too long putting on Halloween make-up, singing along to Paramore, both deluded in thinking that the future would be better for us. We hadn't spoken for a while. The last time was the day before my flight when he asked me to keep in touch and I said I would and then I didn't.

Away from him, in this new country, I cut off bits of myself to fit into a mould of a clique that didn't suit me. I tried to manipulate people who couldn't understand me into loving me, so desperate for a fresh start that I didn't consider all the loose ends I'd left behind. I don't know what my friend was doing during all this time. Perhaps it was something similar. All I know is that he must have been suffering to do what he did.

And he wasn't the first man I'd ever loved, or indeed the first man I'd ever loved who then went on to kill himself, but—as I wish I could tell any teenager, crying naked and lonely between soiled bedsheets—your firsts aren't always as significant as you think.

After my friend's funeral, I lay in my back garden, allowing the black dress to soak in the heat, feeling the sweat gathering underneath my breasts and chafing where armpits met cloth. It's impossible to sleep the night before a funeral. I was so exhausted, reality was fuzzy. I rolled over onto my stomach, resting my head on top of my hands, allowing the sun to burn my legs as much as it desired. Before I slept, I kept my eyes open just long enough to see two white butterflies fluttering around the green and purple flowers, dancing with each other like ghosts, and I wished that I could take a picture before I stopped and wondered, *Who the hell for?* They kissed the petals and so I closed my eyes. I slept long enough to learn that a gentle breeze through summer trees is the most sympathetic alarm clock known to man. The butterflies were gone, but I remembered them and smiled.

I asked myself, *if I am really so cynical, then why does this image bring me so much comfort? Why does a passing remark made two years before and heard through a haze of drunkenness stick with me when I clearly neglect to remember so much that's important? Strange*, I thought. *So strange.*

Blank Face

It doesn't have eyes, but it watches me. I am so unnerved by its stare. I want to say "he" and not "it" because the head is bald and the chest is flat, but there's something inhuman about the way it stares that I'm not quite used to, something so accusing I can't help but feel guilty. I don't know how the artist picked up the chalk and made the non-existent eyes follow me. I stare at it with my notepad and tilt my head, all insincere, just in case someone's looking. People might think I know what I'm doing here if I look thoughtful.

Johnny didn't come today. He doesn't come to school anymore. He would like it here, though. He's been an artist for as long as I can remember, and I can see him adoring this place especially. The walls are huge plates of glass, giving every impression of light and space so it doesn't feel constrained and stuffy like in a normal gallery. It's good for décor and claustrophobia. But no, he isn't here. Johnny's too talented to be here. He doesn't need to go on school trips or get trampled in hallways or draw terrible self-portraits in lessons where you hope the teacher doesn't notice you're hungover. He's already making it, selling work everywhere. His art exhibitions are all over the papers.

The longer I stare at that weird, blank face, where the absent eyes consider me from some distant reality, the harder I find it to breathe, and I'm getting bored of feeling like I'm being watched by something that doesn't really exist. I feel distinctly like it's weighing up my pros and cons and deciding if I deserve to live or not. Am I a real person now? Are these brushstrokes making me edgy and deliberate, or are they messy wastes of canvas? This face knows, as I tilt my head, that I'm faking absolutely everything. It knows how I can't cry anymore. It knows how much I sleep, how much alcohol I drink to justify this. It watches me as I eat, shit, masturbate, shakes its head and makes a note, reminds me that I'm not person enough to rationalise this selfishness. It clocks up my ticket stubs, my sketches, and my empty bottles, and says that maybe, one day, these things might make me a proper person.

I try to look at other things, but the chalked body twists so it can watch me across the room. It won't let me leave. It'll be etched into every darkness now, waiting for me under sheets and eyelids. It won't speak to me but will watch as I sleep another twelve hours, as I eat and grow fatter and sadder and more grotesque like the sculptures it lives with, female sculptures made from bronze with triangle tits and bulging eyes that look infected. I make a note to tell Johnny about the statues later. He'd find them interesting.

The class is heading back to school now. I'm supposed to go back with them for the afternoon's mandatory PE lesson, but I head home instead. This term we're playing football. I hate it so much that I forged a note from my doctor saying that I couldn't participate for risk of sparking a PTSD breakdown. So far no one's questioned it, so on some level it must be believable.

Johnny lies on the bed with his eyes closed. Concentrating, he searches for artistic motivation. His sketchpad is balanced on his chest, and he taps the pencil on it in a consistent, rhythmic thud. When he's like this, in one of his daydreams, I can indulge in staring at him. His long eyelashes, his smooth, pale skin, his breathing so relaxed it's almost mechanical. It's the kind of beauty that makes you want to die.

See, the thing is, I won't cut myself because that hurts, and I've heard that if you're legitimately depressed that's the sort of thing you're supposed to do. I don't want to kill myself; I just don't want to live either. As if he can see into my head, Johnny breaks out of his trance to say, "You know, if I had to die, I think I'd jump off a building for the feeling of temporary flight."

"Yeah?" I ask.

"Yeah." He smiles. "Think of all the space you'd have surrounding you when you fell. It'd be like that entire section of the universe was just for you, if only for a couple of nanoseconds. You wouldn't be some indistinguishable face in the crowd."

"I can understand that. Jumping off something, I mean. Especially if you'd be dead before the impact. But what if you weren't dead when you hit the ground? If you didn't go high enough for the pressure to kill you first and you felt your skull cave in? What if it didn't even kill you right? What if it just turned your brain to mush and you had to lie in a hospital while writers from the Daily Mail shouted about why you should be forced to breathe through a machine forever? What then?"

I look at him.

"I don't know," Johnny says. "You think too much about these things."

"Fuck you," I respond. "You're the one who brought it up."

Johnny's been depressed, I think. Not like me, but actually properly. In Year Eight, he used to carve his girlfriends' names into his arm with a mathematical compass. When they dumped him, he'd cross them out and add some crooked lines to run across his wrist. He always had this compulsion to decorate blank canvasses. I'd watch across the room, making my eyes all big and round, hoping he'd realise how much I cared. I was desperate to save him, but maybe it was because, selfishly, I wanted him indebted to me. He was always better looking than the other boys in our year.

We were friends at home but not in school because he was always with some girl or in some band while I liked to be by myself, but after school when it got dusky and the air smelt heavy and cold, we'd sit on park swings waiting for the streetlights to come on, and he'd tell me everything about his life.

"Abbie totally gets me," he'd say.

"She's very pretty," I'd respond bitterly, and she was. Her lips were full and pouted in a way that echoed Molly Ringwald. She dyed a streak of her hair purple for two days before the school shouted at her and she had to cut it out. But two days was enough. Everyone suddenly realised how edgy she was, even though she still dotted the "I' with a little heart when she wrote her name on exercise books. Immediately, she and Johnny got together.

He drew sketches of her constantly. Even for a twelve-year-old, they were amazing. The teachers thought so, too. All Abbie's girlfriends ooohed and aaaahed over them, and she would sit smiling smugly, knowing that everyone was jealous because she had the pretty boy with the floppy fringe and the brooding, artistic personality.

Then she broke up with him a year later. At the time, it seemed like the most intense break-up of the century, which was impressive because I think The Clash were breaking up around then too. She handed back the sketches he'd drawn of her, and Johnny ripped them up. I told him not to. I said he'd regret it, but he never listened to me.

"It's just too painful to look at her," he said, staring at the end of his shoe as he rocked back and forth on the swing. He wrapped his arm around the chain and bit his lip, and I remember feeling an ache to make him feel better intermingled with anticipation. He listened to The Smiths for a while after that, but he soon got over it and started dating someone else. After Abbie, all his girls were, and still are, background noise to me.

I'm staring at this circle that's meant to be my face. There are about six eyes in it, all of them rubbed out, but I can still see the lines. I can still see they look pissed off at me.

"How can you not get us symmetrical?" they scoff. "Even idiots can draw eyes. Is there anything you can do right?"

No, I think, *no. There's nothing. I'm not pretty. I don't look like Molly Ringwald. Johnny doesn't fancy me, I'm failing maths, I'm useless at sport, I can't handle my drink, and now my stomach's all twisted and nauseous. The only thing I'm good at is art, supposedly, and I can't even draw eyes right.*

My teacher spots me across the room, resting my chin on my hand. He must see that I look despondent, and I want to stop him and say that really, it's fine; it's just the hangover. He leans over my shoulder and looks down at the crumpled, blurry mess.

"Why don't you try it on a new piece of paper?" he says, sympathetically.

"Why? So I can fuck that up, too?"

Detention. An additional hour staring at another blank, judgemental face and the thought rises again like a bubble in my brain, "Is this really how you're gonna spend your life? Do you really deserve to exist?"

I think about Johnny and how he can draw so well he's practically famous. Everyone fancies Johnny. His eyes are completely symmetrical. He's even okay at sports, which is why he went to that football game with his little brother, but I'm not supposed to think about that.

When I leave detention, Abbie's waiting outside. Her eyes are wet, and she's looking at me desperately. I walk straight past her without even thinking.

"Hey," she says. I turn around. "You're friends with Johnny. He told me about you." I hope I don't look too delighted.

"Yeah," I nod. "I'm seeing him tonight."

"I saw in the papers..." she says, gulping.

I can't help but laugh. "I bet you wish you kept his drawings now."

Her face turns chalk white, and as her mouth gapes open, I see her lips trembling. I don't think I've ever seen anyone so angry at me before. Was the break-up really that bad? I guess so because then the tears start spilling down her cheeks.

"Fuck you," she whispers. "Fuck you."

"Can you believe her?" I say to Johnny. "It's like now you're doing well she wants back in." I dip my hand into my bag of crisps and shake my head.

"I'm not doing well, and you know that," Johnny says. I roll my eyes.

"You're too modest. That's your problem."

"Stop," he says. "I'm not doing well."

"No," I say. "No, you're fine. Your art is famous..."

"Please, just listen."

"You're fine. Johnny, you're fine."

And then I'm sobbing, pathetically, again. I'm always doing this, sobbing alone on the plastic, hospital chairs, while the nurses hurry past the open door, knowing that it would be useless to try and comfort someone who doesn't want to be comforted.

Recently, Johnny's parents have been all over the papers. Desperate for the suffering to end, they're bargaining with the courts for euthanasia. I'm bargaining with God for a trade. His life for mine. I wouldn't even question it. There would be no hesitation.

The Hillsborough disaster was over a year ago, but a year isn't long enough for me. Johnny's chest caved in from the pressure of too many people. This broke one of his ribs, which in turn pieced his lung, making Johnny bleed internally. Now, he needs a machine to breathe. They feed him by forcing the food through a tube up his nose. It's still a life. A half-life, sure, but they can't let him go yet. Not yet. Not with his little brother gone, too. But the situation keeps looking hopeless, and they're starting to see things properly.

Johnny will never get to be a professional artist. His face is pale and blank. His eyes are closed, but I feel as though he's watching me, and I know what he's thinking, not what he's saying in my made-up conversations, but what he would be thinking if there was any brain activity left. He'd watch his talent fly away, totally wasted while I ruin sheets of paper with my pointless, messy face. He'd stare at me, begrudgingly.

"I had some potential," he would say, "but you—do you really deserve to exist?"

Ends of the Beck

The clouds create a cocktail with wisps of pink bright as smoked salmon. The autumn day begins to chill. Our afternoon picnic lasted longer than intended. I text Jennifer to let her know that I'll be home late again. My head swims from the warmth of red wine. The taste of brie spread over crackers and black, bitter olives lie at the back of my throat. As he turns around to look at me, I feel my heart beat faster. He hooks his arm through mine, leading me along the wooden path through the trees. I'm grateful to the cold for excusing my blushing cheeks. Richard considers me, smiling mischievously. He stops walking and spins me around to face him, his arms around my waist, and I wonder if this is it, if this will be our moment.

"Rebecca," he starts, and my legs turn to breadcrumbs. I hold his gaze. "How do you feel about getting a little bohemian?"

It's bloody freezing outside, but for once in her life, our Shanade don't have plans on a Saturday. Result! A chance for me to go out instead of looking after the bairn. Don't get me wrong, I love nan-duty, but I still have my youth. I keep telling our Shanade, forty-five int death! She'll be my age one day, and she'll be lucky to have the aid of good genes and peroxide too.

I felt a bit giddy putting on my glad-rags. Barry had texted (no restraint, that one) asking me to wear the leopard top he likes. Cheeky bloody article! I knew I shouldn't wear it out of principle, but it does make me look nice. I've always had a bosom like a shelf, and if you've got it, flaunt it. I'm just glad that I've still got it, to be honest. It was touch and go after having our Shanade, but my girls still managed to bounce back.

Cold as it is, I'll have my vodka Red Bull blanket on soon enough, I'm sure. I take my long coat with the fur round the collar for the walk there in my tottery heels. I kissed our little girl goodnight, and I like to think she understood what was happening, although she still looked at me with a tiny frown as though wondering where the bloody hell I thought I was going. "I'll see you tomorrow morning, Princess," I said.

Our Shanade's too old for kisses now, so I just said, "Right, you. Don't burn the bloody house down," and she rolled her eyes. Right enough to be fair to her, because the day I hear Shanade has tried her hand at cooking is the day I hear a pregnant nun's seen snow in bloody Africa. Before I go, I hear her say, "Have a good time, Mum," because she is a sweetheart really, and I respond, "Aye, don't wait up," and I hear her groan *urghhhhh*. Charming! You'd think I'd told her that I'm planning on coming home covered in snot! I laugh as I close the door behind me.

He's got his arms around me now. I lean against him so that I can stay upright. We've both orchestrated this position to ensure we have the most body-contact possible, I'm sure of it. I'm so nervous that my breath catches in my chest, and I'm worried he can hear my shaking exhales. The swans are gliding beautifully along the water, elegant as dancers. It's meditative being out here, sheltered from the worst of the wind.

I feel my phone buzz and check it, annoyed. A text from Jennifer saying she's got the little ones off to bed. Caitlyn is still having nightmares apparently. Benedict sleeps like a log, so there's no worries there.

"Everything okay?" Rich asks.

"Oh yes, just my daughter letting me know how they all are, you know. Mum-duty. You never get time off."

Richard passes me the hipflask, and I take a swig. It's been so long since I drank whisky. I feel delinquent as we lean against the tree, the sky turning a rich blue now, with a spattering of stars.

I don't want to talk about my children. I'd never be so self-absorbed as to show him pictures. Men are never interested in those kinds of things, but at forty-five (and thankfully looking much younger thanks to a combination of good bones and an *artist* of a beautician), you really do have to be honest about your family situation and all the external baggage it entails. Richard's still a bachelor after all these years. I suppose it makes sense that he's never married before with all his books, his academia, his PhD. He's a poet. Where on earth would he find the time?

He passes me the metal hipflask, and I drink again, feeling the radiator sensation spreading through my bones. It reminds me of being a child on Bonfire night when you're cold on the outside but warm on the inside and ever so happy to be alive.

He holds my gaze as I hand it back to him. The way I'm turning strains my neck, but I don't dare avert my eyes

"You know," he says. "I think you're rather beautiful."

It's nice, our local. It's on the waterfront, so you've got a decent view when you're having a fag. The lights from the flats on t'other side glitter on the water like fairy-lights. Lovely and sparkly! I always wish I could live there. Still, loud as us lot get, maybe not. With the likes of our Barry about, you'd be having sleepless nights even on the top floor! Well, I can't say I'd mind a sleepless night with our Barry.

"Ey up," he says as I wander into the smoking area. "Fancy seeing you here!"

"Now then, trouble," I say reaching forward to kiss him on the cheek. Course, I say hello to all the girls and boys in the same way, so it doesn't look like I'm playing favourites (can't help but notice Sheila's lost an awful lot of weight, and not in a good way. She looks a lot older, and her Pete already smells like a brewery).

"Not seen you about in a while," Katie says.

"Aye, well, you know how it is with a little one at home."

Katie snorts. "I don't know, thank god!" Katie laughs like a horse when she's nervous.

"Oh right, yeah. Lucky one, you are!"

"Don't have to tell me!"

I feel awful for our Katie, really. She always wanted kids, but she'd had two "miscarriages" when she was in her teens and regretted them. I wouldn't trade my girls for anything like, but course you can't say that to Katie. We all find ways of coping with our lot.

"Right, you need a drink!" Barry says.

"Don't be silly. I can get it."

"What kind of gentleman would I be?" he asks, and I laugh because there's no one who looks less like a gentleman than our Barry in his paint-splattered jeans and old parka jacket. God, he's handsome, though. He's lost all his hair, God love him, but he can pull it off. You can pull off being a baldy if you've got a nice face.

"G'on then. I'll have a chardonnay," I say, stroking his arm and hoping that it signifies more than just a friendly thanks. "Large!" I shout after him as he goes back into the pub. He holds up his hand to show he's heard, then turns around and grins. I feel a little jolt in my belly, as if I'm a silly schoolgirl. *Christ*, I think, feeling my cheeks go red. *It's been a while.*

Youth spills from my centre, a flood of energy and libido burning the inside of my skin. How had it started? The open-mouth kiss, the hot breath on my neck? The hand slipping underneath my top, cupping a breast? It was none of these and all at once. I crave him.

The hand reaching down, the angle curved, and himself, stiffening against the cold.

My flesh is free and covered in goose-bumps, my ankle rubbing against the ground, but I barely mind the filth that will attach itself to me. It feels beautiful and natural and strong.

I'm sure it never felt this good before. As soon as it's over, I lay my head on his chest. His long woollen coat covers us both, and I am smiling.

Now obviously, back in the day, we'd've got a taxi, but with our Shanade, there's no chance of that happening. She'll still be up watching rubbish about ghosts or celebrities who've injected too much shite into their face and had it all collapse.

I don't know how it happened, really. Usually, I've got a bit of class. I noticed Barry nursing his pint for hours, the same one through four or five fags, taking sips instead of glugs. Pete was already off his head when I came in, so it was no surprise when Sheila had to drag him home quite soon after, (which seems to be happening more and more, god bless her. I've told her she wants rid). Then Katie did what Katie does and got off with a barman who was almost twice her age and no prince from what I could see, but who am I to stop her?

Then it was just us.

I said, "You've hardly drank tonight," and he said, "Aye, neither have you," and we looked at each other and his hand was on my knee, and I dunno whether I batted my eyelashes in a certain way or what, but he looked down and said, "Nice top," and before you knew it, I was all over him, my tits pushed into his chest, my hand on his back, sloppily kissing like teens at a bus stop. And now this.

If you sneak off down the canal, there's a place under the flyover and god, it were cold, but Barry's hands were warm enough when he was kissing me and his hand were under my chin, and before you knew it, I'd managed to position myself on the wall, and my pants were moved to the side and ohhhhhhhhhhhh.

Oh, I suppose I needed this. He got himself out (a quick unzip job, we never had the time) and it was warm and nice and it didn't hurt and then it was over. I can't say I felt very sophisticated. But when Barry lifted up my chin and said, "I like you, you know," I felt my heart beat fast again and kissed him softly on the cheek. He gave me a hand down, and I felt his cum drip down my leg. I'd have to pop back home to shower. It was only a short walk, just past the station. He dropped us off. Snogged us outside the front door.

"Night, night, you," he said.

"Yeah, yeah, get yourself off to bed."
I smiled.

It's funny how love can make you feel like
a right ol' bloody tart.

Too soon it always ends. The night fades
from blue to inky black, and the stars called
me home. Caitlyn had another nightmare
and woke up crying for me. I left it a while
but soon the calls were insistent.

Richard walks me back through the
woods towards the dodgy end of town and
calls me a taxi. He holds me in his arms as
we wait for it to arrive, and when I leave, he
kisses me on the cheek.

I rest my forehead against the glass
window in the back seat of the taxi. The
streetlamps here are few and far between.
Soon, we reach the main street where people
stumble down in large, howling groups,
cackling like witches. Hen-dos and pink
tutus and ambulances parked outside of
bars. A woman in a leopard-print shirt and
faux-fur coat grinds her hips against a bald
man by the station, and I can't help but feel
like alcohol brings the animal out of common
people. I close my eyes, my head still spinning from euphoria, but now I am sick and
tired. I look forward to my bed.

The trees grow taller, the houses farther apart, and I know I am reaching home. The meter keeps on ticking, leaving everything I felt tonight further and farther behind.

New Harem Pants

She turned up late and in ludicrous trousers, the crotch dangling almost to her knees, her curly, grey hair swept back with a rainbow sweatband, looking more like she belonged at Glastonbury than a family Sunday dinner.

"My darling boy! Sorry I'm late. Jazzercise ran over," she said, which at least explained the sour aroma of powdery roll-on deodorant. She kissed me on the cheek with a loud "mwah." It pained me when my mother kissed so nonchalantly, using pet names and big smiles as though she hadn't spent my childhood in a perpetual state of chilliness. I swore she only did it to show me up for the liar that I *wasn't*.

"It's fine. The vegetables might be soggy, that's all," I said.

"Now, where's my favourite girl?" she called out loudly, and Harriet raced down the stairs in quick little thumps, wearing quirky, tortoise socks that she was far too old for.

"Grandma!" she called out, with no sense of pretence, and I had to refrain from rolling my eyes.

"There she is! Now, let me look at you," my mother replied, holding her at arm's length. Harriet was almost, but not quite, as thin as her mother, and recently she'd shaved her head into some ludicrous, Mohican-type style, a short fringe slicked back with gel atop an overly eye-linered face. "Oh, you get taller by the day. Doesn't she look so pretty with all that hair off her face, Charles?"

"I'm not an expert on hairstyles," I replied, which was true. I hadn't even known I'd inherited my mother's curly hair until my father died. Before that she always wore it in such a tight bun that it was impossible to tell anything about it except that it must have been giving her a headache.

And I hated my daughter's hair. It was clearly done as a way to protest conformity, but why? It was hard enough for Harriet with her mother the way she was without her taking extra pains to isolate herself.

"Men, ey?" my mother tutted in a pathetic attempt at comradery. "Useless."

"Right, well, this should be ready now," I said, shimmying past them into the kitchen.

"Fantastic, I am starved! The girls have been taking me to the farmer's market on the weekends, and of course, they're all vegan so I feel just terrible about wandering over to the butcher's stall or the fish market, but I'll tell you what, after a week of cauliflower stew, I am *hankering* for a good bit of roast beef."

"It's lamb," I replied, wondering when my mother suddenly gained "girls" that took her to farmer's markets.

"Well, even better," she said.

"Smells great, Dad."

"Thank you, sweetheart. Wine, Mum? Red or white?"

"No thank you, dear. A tea would just be lovely, though. Especially if you have green."

"We don't."

"Oh, well, an English Brekky will do nicely, then."

I slotted the bottle back into the wine-rack. I knew I couldn't drink alone without side-eyes and comments. It seemed my mother wanted to deprive me of even the slightest comfort. I jealously watched the girls dig into the meal I'd cooked while I stood waiting for the kettle to boil.

"So, tell me everything, lovey. How's school?" my mother said.

"Fine," Harriet replied. "I've nearly finished now. I have my GCSEs next month."

"Oh, wow! And have you been revising?"

I smirked. The way Harriet "revised" con-sisted of staring at the telly with a pile of test-pa-pers and an open book in front of her, insisting that she knew what she was doing and that by coming in to oversee I was "distracting her."

"A little," she said. "But I don't really need good grades anyway for the apprenticeship I want to do."

I bristled. "Well, actually, we still need to discuss that." The kettle clicked off and I poured the hot water into the mug. I didn't wait for it to brew before adding the milk, thinking that if my mother insisted on making my life difficult, she may as well not enjoy it.

"Oh perfect, lovely," she said as I handed it to her at the table, and I winced. It wasn't perfect or lovely. It was the colour of a bathroom stall. "So, what is it you want to do, my dear?"

"There's a guy who runs a tattoo studio in town. He's seen my drawings and said he'd take me on as an apprentice. It's great money," she rushed on quickly, clearly more for my benefit than my mother's, "and I've always really liked drawing. I can start straight away and save up and I could even get my own flat when I'm eighteen."

"Well, how very entrepreneurial, pet."

"Really?" Try as I might, I couldn't keep the indignity out of my voice. "You're supporting this?"

"Well, it's best to allow children the freedom to branch out into creativity, surely?"

I clenched my teeth in the way which worried my dentist and which I had to pretend I only did in my sleep. I remembered how much I loved to play the clarinet. I was one of the only ones in the school band who hadn't been given professional lessons, but I'd taught myself with the

second-hand, dusty model left in the music cup-
board, all the way from the recorder playing "Hot
Cross Buns" up until I mastered "Greensleeves"
on a beautiful model with silver buttons. My
music teacher had encouraged me with the correct breathing techniques, even giving up his free
time on breaks to help me, which was good of
him considering my parents never paid him a
penny. I remember his blonde hair, his serious
grey eyes as he watched me play, and the brightly
coloured, tightly fitted jumpers he always wore
over his work shirts.

But it wasn't meant to be. Despite my evident promise, my parents were never going to
fork out for the proper equipment, and when it
came to sports day and the opportunity for the
band to practice our school song, my parents
were ashamed.

"Why can't you just," my father suggested,
"play sports like all the other boys, huh? It's sports
day. Run a fucking race."

And as much as this, in and of itself, may
have constituted as justification enough for the
therapy, the image that hurt me most was not that
of his beetroot face, his pained inflections, but the
cold and sternly disappointed expression of my
mother lingering behind him, promising there
would be unspoken repercussions and for what,
I ask? Playing the clarinet?

And now here she was at my kitchen table, supposedly the same woman, proudly encouraging

my daughter to slip into degeneracy in a disingenuous show of encouragement.

"Well, I think the whole idea's bloody ridiculous," I said. As though in solidarity, my knife scraped against the plate and Harriet flinched in response. She placed her fork down and slumped back against the chair. My mother eyed her, worriedly.

"Now, I think before we carry on with dinner, we should address the elephant in the room," she said.

Oh God. If there was anything my mother excelled at, it was picking the worst possible moment to bring up a sensitive issue.

"Let's leave it for now, hey?" I said. "Just enjoy the nice roast."

"Darling, I don't think there's any good in refusing to talk about these things. Quite clearly you're both upset."

Harriet smiled at her weakly. I dropped down my cutlery and it clattered on the plate. I supposed none of us would be able to enjoy the meal now.

"I know that your mother is unwell at the moment, and I just wanted to offer my help with anything you need."

"We're fine for money," I said.

"I didn't mean money," she said tightly. She turned to Harriet. "My poor girl, you must be worried sick."

"Yeah." Harriet shrugged petulantly. "I guess. She's just so thin…"

"I don't think there's any point in talking about your mother behind her back, is there?"

"Charles, don't be so difficult," my mother replied, and for a second, I saw a shadow of the woman I grew up with, that same harsh tone and furrowed brow. "Your wife is suffering, and the problem isn't just going to go away the more we ignore it."

"She'll be fine," I said. "We've got the best care possible for her situation."

"She hates it there. She wants to come home," Harriet said, directing this at my mother as a clear way of undermining me.

"Well, that's where she'll stay until she cooperates..."

"With who, Dad?" Harriet asked, her eyes suddenly ablaze. "Is she stuck there until she cooperates with the doctors? Or with you? She wants a divorce..."

"Your mother doesn't know what she wants," I added. "She's very sick. Look," I took a deep breath, "you don't need to worry about us divorcing, love. She was very unwell when she said that. I'm sure she'll change her mind when she's better."

Harriet looked like she wanted to spit in my eye, and I knew that if my mother wasn't sitting opposite me, I might have been tampted to slap her, but I refused to give my mother the satisfaction, refused to let her see me use the same abusive methods she had.

"Oh dear," my mother muttered almost to her-self. "I didn't realise how bad it quite was…"

"It's *not*," I found myself growling, and had to pause before I continued, "all that bad."

"It's basically medieval, Dad. You've got her all locked up…"

"She's anorexic, Harriet."

"She's on a fucking hunger strike, more like it."

"Alright, I think we all need to just calm down," my mother said, using her "yogic voice," which always made me want to break plates against the wall.

"Don't you dare talk to me like that," I directed this at Harriet, but I knew it was intended for the both of them.

"Listen," my mother said, raising her voice just slightly. She placed one hand on Harriet's and one on mine, stretching her arms wide. I kept my fist clenched, refusing to allow for the insincere tenderness. "Obviously, this is a horrible situation. Harriet, darling, your mother is poorly. She needs to stay in the hospital until she's better. There's no denying that." Harriet squirmed on the chair but nodded. I hated that. How often had I tried to tell her the same thing only to be ignored? I wish I could've pointed this out, but my interfering mother was already moving on. "Charles," she said. "Rebecca is clearly not in her right mind right now, but if she wants to leave, you must let her. The heart wants what it wants…"

"Oh Jesus Christ," I said, flinging her hand off me. "What kind of cliché is that?"

"A true one," she continued firmly. "I know this is painful…"

"I've had enough of this." I stood up from the table, but it suddenly occurred to me I had nowhere to go. This was my house. *She* was the intruder. And yet I was being forced to leave. The injustice of it all strengthened my resolve, and I knew I had to get out before I blew up.

"Oh darling, where are you going?" she called after me, but I just slammed the front door behind me. I checked my pockets. I had my car keys but no wallet. It wasn't the worst it could be, but it wasn't the best either. I longed to find a pub where I could sit quietly in a corner drinking glass after glass of wine without anyone bothering me, but with no wallet, I was left in the lurch. I decided to go for a drive to clear my head, to get rid of the anger that had been piling up all afternoon. That was what they did on the television, right? There must be some truth in its effectiveness.

I thought of what my therapist had called my "happy place." The beach near my old school, no doubt. I used to go there when I didn't want to go to my lessons. Even when it was cold, I found the salty air refreshed and warmed me from the inside out.

On the way there, through the winding roads where the city cleared to old tat shops and beachy souvenirs, I thought about the time I came with him. We were in sixth form and there was no real reason for us to have to attend school on a sports day (I had long ago given up my spot in the school band), so we wandered out to the beach, taking pride in our slight, inconsequential rebellion. It was a hot day in July, but because it was a Monday, the beach was mostly empty. We stripped down to our shorts and waded into the sea up to the waist until the waves were so biting cold, we had to make a hasty retreat and spend some time drying out in the sun, our heads resting on our rucksacks. I still remember how hot his hands felt, how salty the kiss. When I got home, I took a shower and washed away the sand that stuck and itched between my thighs. Obviously, I never told anyone. I didn't want to be beaten, but they found out anyway and I was. My mother was a dab hand with a switch. I suppose she'd say it was a different time back then. She did reflect on her old opinions with a sanctimonious sense of shame, which she clearly believed absolved her from any wrongdoing. I wondered why the beach remained my happy place when it was sodden with so much conflict. I suppose that even pain can't taint those moments of euphoria.

On a Sunday afternoon, it wasn't quite the same. There wasn't the same seclusion, and since my youth, they'd added too many loud fairground rides. There were still the usual suspects ready to make the place look untidy; fat families wandering along with 99s and Staffordshire terriers, teenagers in hoodies hugging each other as screaming nonsense played from their phone speakers. Even when I sat on the rock I once used to regularly perch upon (the rock I had

labelled *my* spot as a young man), I felt conspic-
uous and uncomfortable. Paranoia convinced me
that everyone was staring at me and worst of all
seeing me, knowing where I'd come from, what
exactly it was I was running from. The seagulls
squawked above me, and I wished that I could
join them.

Back home I imagined the crying scenes, the
way my mother would be hugging Harriet and
rubbing up and down her back, the comforting
tone, and worse still, the way she would defend
my actions while continuing to undermine me in
a way that was petty and contrived but still made
her appear angelic by comparison. Eventually, I
would have to leave and go back to my normal,
miserable existence, but I couldn't just yet. Not
yet. Instead, I watched toddlers build sandcastles
only to smash them with their spades until the
families wandered home and dusk settled over
the horizon, and I'd bored myself for long enough
to know the feelings I had didn't matter anymore.

The Sudden
Appearance of Bears

I tell myself that I hadn't wanted Mother to die. It had been a cold winter then, few animals and fewer crops. We ate the bark from trees, grimaced at the way it crunched in our mouths, splinters sticking in our throats. The others told us that Siberia was the harshest place to survive on earth. I asked them if that made us the harshest people. I never really got a response.

We all missed Mother greatly, that is true. After all, it was her warmth that made life so bearable. She would sit with me and Pevunya as we patched up our clothes while Father was away hunting. Back then, he would often be gone for days, and I never understood exactly how he hunted. He called it "men's work," and naively, I'd believed him. Of course, Pevunya and I could never hunt. There was always too much to do around the home to keep everyone warm. Mother taught us that the men needed warmth to keep their strength up when there wasn't enough food to eat. Mother had us believe she could survive entirely on warmth.

That was many years ago. Our family stayed hidden until the others found us. Now my entire family is dead. First, Mother, starved, eaten. Pevunya and Medvezhonok, their organs slowly failing, their skin colour changing. Then Father. Father was the hardest blow. I mean it when I say I hadn't wanted him to die.

The sky is blue as I bury him, but the soil has turned to ice. The trees seem duller as they surround me, visibly grey despite the sun. The others insisted that it was worth the journey. They have this strange idea that Father would have wanted them to be here, but I wish that they wouldn't try to help. I want to scream at them as they shiver so dramatically, shaking out their arms like bedsheets. I want to tell them that it's their fault he is dead, their fault they're all dead, but of course, I cannot say this. They wouldn't understand anyway. My Russian was never fine-tuned enough for their ears, and to this day, I find myself painfully repeating things yet remaining misunderstood. The others found us children simple-minded, said we chattered like birds in trills and coos. I suppose it was fair of them to think that. We never understood them much either.

As sisters, Pevunya and I would hold each other at night and try to sleep, hoping for dreams. Dreams were the best parts of those winter nights.

We whispered to each other in gentle, sleeping voices, speaking about what we hoped would come, and then in the morning about what had happened. It seemed that my sister could manipulate her mind, force herself to dream kind things in a way I always envied.

"I dreamt that there were rabbits," she once told me, "and you and Mother cooked them in a stew, and we ate like kings." She grinned at me, and I smiled too, embarrassed that my dreams were less concrete. Pevunya always dreamt of the house, of cooking and food. She never dreamt of anything that she didn't already know. I felt resentful when I had to tell my stories, and she couldn't understand them.

"The sky was purple," I once told her. "And I was me, except I wasn't. At one point, I was Father. And for days we walked through the snow looking for a deer, except, when it had finally grown too tired to run, we realised it wasn't a deer at all. It was a bear that reached to the moon and spoke to me in a language only I understood. Its words came out in green smoke and shocked me so deeply that I chased myself back towards the house, but the house had been replaced by strange, metal mountains, reaching higher than the trees, and I knew it to be a city. I ran in to search for you, but I realised that it was burning to the ground and soon we would all burn with it."

"How sad," Pevunya responded. "What did the bear say in the green smoke?"

"I don't know. I just know that I felt scared."

"Yes, well, you shouldn't tell Medvezhonok. He will take your ideas and spread them as his own. You know how Mother and Father feel about images of hellfire."

"Of course, I will not tell him," I'd snapped, irritated that we'd move onto practicalities so quickly. Pevunya was right, though. I hated watching my little brother scolded. Mother thought he needed to be more of a man, but Father always intervened. *Allow him to stay young,* he would say. *He will grow and learn in time.* And Medvezhonok printed images in the snow with his wooden galoshes. It was a shame I couldn't confess my dreams to him. He spoke too much, but I was sure that he would understand, perhaps better than our sister could at least.

Now, I know that I was wrong. I was wrong about the cities. They were more like grey rectangles with lights which gave you headaches, and I was wrong about Pevunya, too. I would realise when we were in the others' world that she understood me better than anyone. Now that Father is gone, I wonder if I will ever be truly understood again. Perhaps the bear from my dreams can understand me. Perhaps one day I will speak the language of green smoke.

I stand over my father's body and search for some emotion. I crave some sense of solitude or fear but notice nothing. It's possible that the initial sense of loss has never really gone away. Perhaps it is now so much a part of me that I fail to notice it, the way you cannot notice the bite of the snow when your fingers are already frozen. I watch the others, working pathetically with their shovels to cover his body, worrying about the sudden appearance of bears and the rapidly setting sun. Somehow, this helps me find some sense of feeling. I am glad not to be one of them. I am glad to be alone.

I wish I could return to that time, before Mother died, only I'd be the age that I am now. I'd do it just to tell myself that I was far more competent than they ever gave me credit for. I'd throw my arm around my skinny frame and say that when they were all dead and gone, I'd have more to eat than I could ever imagine. I'd tell myself that there is less to share, and weapons with which to hunt. I'd say that one day, I will wander in the dark without apprehension. I will live to be brave and not turn away from that which I fear. There are many things I wish that I could tell myself. I wonder if it would've changed a thing.

I hadn't wanted siblings to die, and I say this with complete sincerity. They called it kidney failure, but I know that they were wrong. It was their world that killed them. Their world with its greed. People had more food than they could eat and owned everything. What do you do when you don't have to work to survive? How do you spend your days? There's only so much time someone can dwell on dreams.

I wonder what Pevunya felt like lying in their hospital, whiter than the snow because it was so stainless. It smelled inhuman, that place, and their chemicals failed to help. She grew weaker, sicker. I held her hand as she passed and told her that I remembered what the bear was saying now. It wasn't really words but a warning, and I never should have run. I wasn't sure if she could hear me then, and they never really learned to understand me when I spoke the way I spoke to her, the way we spoke as children like twinned songbirds. I didn't want them to understand.

When Mother died all those decades ago, I'd convinced myself that I was devastated, but it's difficult to grieve on an empty stomach. When you're full, the emotions grip you completely and your mind is engaged with nothing but the constant, unshakable sense of loss.

Today, I woke to bury Father. I did not feel my stomach twist and drop, possibly because it's never untwisted since those weeks in the hospital, chained to weak, plastic chairs.

I recall the numbness and the constant nausea. Was it their chemicals that caused it? I had once asked Father, but he couldn't answer me. He stared forward, his elbows resting on his knees, his hands together in what I could have called prayer if he weren't so silent, and his eyes so open. "Father, do you feel it? Do you feel the sickness in your stomach, too? I feel it beneath the fire in my lungs. It's hard to breathe, isn't it, Father? Father, are you not breathless?" He never responded, and now I wonder if I really said the thoughts aloud.

My poor, sweet Medvezhonok. There simply aren't words. He jumped into that new world wide-eyed and accepting, laughing when things didn't feel like the texture he'd imagined. Medvezhonok never screamed or grimaced when the new sensations reached his tongue. Trust was always his problem. He trusted too much; that was all.

I consider the cross that marks Father's grave. The grave was quick to fill, and I am hungry. My hunger is a privilege I think Father deserves. The others stand around the grave. As the snow begins to fall, I can see the panic settling behind their eyes. They are worried they won't make it home, but they have the decency not to complain too loudly, surrounded by the tentativeness the others always have when they perceive that I am grieving.

"We must go soon if we want any chance of getting back," one says. "The sun is setting after all, and our supplies are hardly adequate to stay the night."

I see that they are right. The sky is turning purple, and the outline of the moon is creeping through the drifting clouds. I know a quiet storm is coming. I hope the cross is large enough and will not end up buried; it's only a gentle scattering now, but soon the cautious drops will turn to sobs. I look forward to the furs in the cabin. It means something to know there are still things to look forward to.

"You go on now," I tell them. They hesitate, look to each other as though I will be easy to convince, but I shake my head. "Go on."

I watch them recede down the slope, getting smaller and smaller, ant people burdened by the weight of their goods. They turn around to point. They are surprised, I hope, to see my silhouette still watching, supported by the purple sky. The snow travels diagonally, peppering my frozen cheeks, but my eyes stay open. I will not turn away.

Carnival

My first memory, you ask? Well, I suppose in here you do get bored with normal chitchat, particularly when nothing exciting ever occurs here. I used to hate the drudgery, but now I've grown to accept and even embrace it. There's something comforting in relying so heavily on routine. All the same, delving back into those memories of childhood, so unaffected by our adult concern about the passage of time, can be nothing short of a delight. And so, I suppose, we shall indulge. My first memory, you ask... Well, yes.

Once,, as a treat, my parents took me to the travelling circus. It pains me that my first memory is so commonplace as to verge on the cliché, but unfortunately, the circus it was. Through the hazy curtain of time, I can still recall the huge gazebos in bright, primary colours, the white-painted faces of clowns looming over my small frame, and the constant squeaking and popping of long, tumescent balloons. It was in the years before anyone was concerned with animal protection, and the distinct tang of elephant dung tickled my nose.

It's difficult to say how much of my recollection is genuine reality and how much is a collage of various television shows, films, posters, and literature that altogether have created this vivid reminiscence. I was perhaps four or five, although I might have been older. It was a blinding hot day, likely to be August if I wasn't mistaken, close to my birthday when treats like these would usually occur. The sun reflected harshly off the white stripes of the circus tents, accosting my eyes in such a way that I held my hand to my brow almost constantly, shielding my already limited perspective. I recall the sticky sweat behind my knees and a dryness in my mouth that made me whine aloud for orange squash.

Escaping from the vortex of children and clowns, cartoonish and disturbing in their unrelenting happiness, my family and I took shelter from the dizzying heat in one of the many gazebos. We stepped through the flapping doors and were dramatically plunged into darkness. I was led by my mother towards the tiered seats and was relieved to feel the coldness of the metal on my bare legs as I sat. With wide-eyed curiosity, I took in my surroundings.

Dangling above the centre of the circular stage, two strips of red and purple fabric hung like undrawn curtains, crumpling against the dusty floor. The ceiling peaked up to a point and I could barely see the extent of its height. As another family entered the tent, they peeled the opening aside, and the flashing lights from fairground rides hit the corner of my eye, causing a staccato, rainbow migraine. I closed my eyes for a moment, indulging in the rest I was allowed in the sanctuary of this non-spectacle, and when I opened them again, I noticed her. She was seated on the scaffolding, her legs wound casually around the fabric. I should have known it was not wind but her kicks which caused the silky strips to wave like river currents.

I had always presumed that the act of tight-rope walking would be dull. After all, I could walk perfectly well in a straight line by myself, and ignorant as I was about the concept of balance and the danger of gravity, I didn't imagine it could be much harder from up in the air. But seeing the girl up there, swinging her legs so casually beneath her, inspired the shock of vertiginous fear to leap up in my little chest.

Again, I cannot be sure if the image I retain of her is correct (my parents, for example, claim that she was blonde!), or if I've allowed my deepest fantasies to taint the truth as drops of lemon infect a freshly poured gin, but please indulge me in describing what must have been my first ever encounter with true, exceptional beauty. Glitter was crusted around her eyes and up her cheekbones, she shimmered like a night star, and her lips had been painted a red which conflicted deeply with the rest of her juvenile attire. As a child, anyone from the age of twelve or so was considered very much "adult" to me, and in hindsight, I realise I have no idea how old she might have been. Her wild red frizz of hair was tied in two bunches. Her outfit was striped black and blue, tight Lycra across the arms and chest, before exploding into tutu-ed extravagance from the waist down. She looked side to side absent-mindedly from her perch as the scant audience settled in front of her. I saw her pop a bubble of mint-white chewing gum and was impressed by her uninterested façade and the bravery it must have indicated.

Before I could so much as catch her eye, another little girl noticed her nesting up high and called up to her parents with a dramatic point of the finger.

"Look, look! Up there!"

Heads turned so fast one might have presumed the audience was hearing bomber planes. The magic girl waved slightly and blew them all a kiss, staining her palm with her cherry red lips. The crackly sound of a record player began with jaunty vaudevillian music, and the circus master made his appearance in white leather, which must have suffocated him in that heat. He had made-up one of his eyes, but not the other, and his dark beard and tall top-hat seemed to accentuate rather than disguise his shortness of stature. He spoke in a surprisingly deep voice when he reached the microphone.

"Ladies and Gentlemen, are you ready for a show?"

We cheered and clapped, although the emptiness of the crowd seemed to undermine the excitement of the moment.

"Come on, I can barely hear you. I said, are you ready for a show?!"

A few whistles and shrieks were added to the general cheer, but again, it seemed somewhat pathetic when considering how slight the crowd was in comparison to the soaring heights of the gazebo and the frail girl above us.

"Now, that's more like it! Ladies and Gentlemen, boys and girls, let me introduce you to our main event. She's sleek, she's sly, and boy, can she fly. Please put your hands together for Ms. Magpie!"

Again, a little pattering of clapping that in my impolite and ignorant childish state I didn't participate in, instead staring open-mouthed and gormless at the performer in expectation of her leaping from the scaffolding and zooming around the room like a fairy. Instead, she simply wrapped the pieces of cloth round the creases of her knees before flinging herself backwards from her metal throne. I heard a gasp emitting from my mother as the girl cascaded downwards in graceful rolls before landing upside down, her legs bending at an odd angle. I saw the muscles bulging in her arms in a way that seemed to contradict with her femininity. I had little interest in the strong men, but her flexibility and mindfulness seemed nothing short of magical, a control and certainty in the self that I could never have possessed. She pointed her toes and separated her legs slowly, turning them like hands on a clock, perfectly straight and poised, flipping herself into upside-down splits. I noticed with fondness the way that she could manipulate her body to seemingly do anything she pleased, but her bunches still drooped beneath her rebelliously. It was reassuring to understand there were some things beyond her control.

Many counsellors have since explained to me that my fondness for her bunches in no way could have predicted, or indeed caused, the tearing of the purple strip of fabric while Ms. Magpie was suspended in her precarious position. You can imagine my horror as we witnessed our magpie's exceptional, spine-snapping fall from grace.

As is often the case in moments of extreme tragedy, I don't quite recall the twisted body or the sound of breaking bones. Instead, I find myself recollecting the chaotic screams and gasps of the crowd, the ending of the jaunty vaudevillian racket with a comical (and overused, I find) record scratch, the grasping of my head by my mother as she shielded my eyes. Psyche-altering childhood experiences are so often cut short, interrupted by the chests of mothers as the back of our heads are held in their hands.

Travelling home was quiet, as was perhaps to be expected. There was no talk of an alternative treat, which disappointed me. The usual mutterings of, "What did you like? Did you have a nice time?" did not occur.

It's odd that this whole memory is so clearly branded into my mind's eye. Too often what we perceive as authentic childhood memories are in actuality just stories we've been told and have pasted into settings that we believe best befits them. My parents never mentioned the incident at the travelling circus again, supposedly hoping that the trauma would move on like the bumper cars and clowns, the airguns and hook-a-ducks, along to the next town to be forgotten about except as a mirage, a jumbled haze of sun-stroke and euphoria. I heard them tell the neighbours in muted whispers about "something awful," describing the sound of the snap when "the blonde girl fell from her rope," the clink of glasses and hands rifling through peanut bowls, myself seated secretly on the carpet upstairs listening from the banister.

After this incident, I always found it comforting to feel the broken bones of tiny birds who I had managed to salvage from fallen nests, the rodents who would attempt to nip through my thick gardening gloves. It was a long-held family belief that I had always had a propensity for the natural world.

I wanted to see from what height it would be possible for something to survive, but birds flew away, and cats are far too malleable to act as an accurate gauge, so what could be expected except for me to drag those girls from lift-door to windowsill, encouraging them to spill forward from the ledges like dandelion seeds blown about in spring.

Now I find it such a shame that here my time outside is so limited. The hour-a-day walks are barely sufficient enough to serve as proper exercise, although they are a tremendous opportunity for self-reflection. After all, it allows us all to have these kinds of chats. So, I suppose that's my earliest memory. Why do you ask?

Pitchforks and Vicodin

"I had a friend kill himself over some bitch who didn't want him."

- Eminem, "Stan," 2000

There were too many voices and none of them were listening to me. I thought everyone could hear them, so I spoke about them openly, but no. Had I known better perhaps I might have made an attempt to hide it, but I learned too late that this was something abnormal. Too many things about me fell into that category: abnormal. Unmarried. Old. Alone. And then the voices. I suppose this was my destiny, really.

The flames don't "lick" as people say. Instead, they melt the skin around my ankles. My flesh drips like wax, shrivelling and falling away. Before, I promised not to scream, but it proves impossible to avoid. Sweat and tears mingle on my face and my hands are burning. The fire climbs up my dress. There is no point struggling, but I feel certain I can't cope with this for one more second. It is worse than their torture, worse than anything I've ever felt before. I pray for the lord to take me. I hope that if I am reborn, it is into a more forgiving world.

"For men, this is a difficult conversation to have and sadly many women can fail to pick up on underlying clues."

- CPD Online College Base, 2020

I buried another child today. It never gets easier. I've reached a level of guilt that only a mother can achieve. A thought crept up on me this morning as unavoidably as a sudden fit of coughing: *At least there's one less mouth to feed.*

The children don't have this guilt. The younger ones are openly gleeful about the prospect of more space in their bed, more food in their belly. They aren't quite old enough to understand that they should learn to hide this desperation, should have the decency to stand on ceremony and pretend, at least, to mourn. Little Caitlyn cries. I know it's genuine because she doesn't cry with a gaping mouth and panicked shriek like the others do when they need my attention. Instead, she sits quietly, her sewing on her lap as the tears drip onto the fabric. Sniffs escape her intermittently. It's heart-breaking to see. She's young, but she adored the baby. I remember her spoon-feeding him, taking extra care not to let the porridge fall onto his makeshift bib. That was until he began rejecting all the food, spitting up whatever tiny pieces he managed to swallow. At that point, my breasts had dried up. I don't know how. Perhaps even my body knew that there wasn't enough for all of us. But then, that can't be true, or it wouldn't keep happening.

My husband should have been at the funeral, but he had to work. *There's still the others alive,* he explained to me, *and we still need to eat.* He's right. I don't know how he manages it, but when he comes home covered in grime and grease, black around the face and aching from head to foot, he still finds time for love and comfort, still manages to hold me close and tell me how much he loves me. A part of me dreads the proximity, but at least it keeps me warm on freezing nights. The children have each other, but when I'm left alone, I sleep right by the hearth, so close that I often burn my feet and end up a dusty black all over.

My breasts are sore now. I haven't bled in many weeks. The nausea has started again. I know what all this means. I was sure the last one would kill me, and the midwife said I only narrowly escaped with my life. At least Caitlyn might be happy to know she'll soon have a replacement.

"What I'm discussing here is the immediate reduction in a man's quality of life when he associates with a female."

- MGTOW Forum, 2021

I used to stare at the wall every day and wish that I was dead, but thanks to my new medication, I stare at the wall every day and feel nothing. I started out on 50mg, but now I'm up to 200. It feels like floating. I don't really even need to sleep anymore, but when I told my husband that, he laughed and said it was nonsense, that he'd seen me napping angelically on the sofa when he came home from work. So, I suppose I must sleep sometimes. He doesn't know, however, that I can't sleep at night. Even with the Vicodin, I find myself wandering around our den, stroking the polished surfaces like a ghost observing the site of its own demise. If I were to die, how would I go, I wonder? Death by ironing? Lifestyle magazine overdose?

The washing machine and the dishwasher are both switched on and loud in that mechanic, gushing way which gives everything a dreamlike quality. The baby is asleep. Or maybe she isn't. Maybe she's crying and I can't hear her over the sound of all our shiny, new appliances. I don't really want to hear her since there's not much I can do to soothe her. She'll have to learn to cry herself out one of these days. My mother said that's how she did it with me.

I tongue the gap at the back of my mouth. When I was pregnant, I lost a back molar. They say that for every baby you have you lose a tooth. Too many children will destroy a smile, absolutely. I don't want any more. The doctor suggested that because of my situation it might be good to get my tubes tied, but my husband said no.

"She's fine," he scoffed. "If anything, she's just bored."

I suppose that's true. So often I find myself pacing this place. A large colonial, I have no right to be unhappy. I've tried to talk to Roy about it. I tell him I feel claustrophobic, that I always find myself struggling to breathe, feeling entangled in a homespun web of laundry lines and apron strings. He tells me that when he gets promoted, we'll move somewhere bigger.

But the pills help. Everything blurs a little. They help me dream even while I'm awake, dozing away on empty Thursday mornings. There's a pile of laundry on the side that I know I have to iron. I don't remember my mother ever ironing my father's shirts, but I suppose that's the benefit of marrying rich and not having to work. I know I'm lucky. I live comfortably. Pearl earrings for Christmas, the diamond engagement ring. I go to the salon to get my hair dyed every six weeks. Blondes have more fun, after all.

I take Roy's shirt and lie it flat on the board. I was never an expert on home economics, but now I'm realising what a fool I was not to listen to Mrs. Becker. I hated that bitch with her high-pitched voice and her grey, curly hair, standing five foot nothing in stockinged feet and using that as an excuse to justify her "hard taps" with the wooden spoon. The steam from the iron rises and hisses like an angry cat. I place it on the shirt, and I don't know… I suppose I thought that I was ironing, but after lifting it back up I saw that I hadn't moved the thing at all. I'd just burned a horrible black triangle into one of Roy's best work shirts. Before the pills, that might have been enough to make me cry, but now I just laugh. Of course, he'll be angry. He's always angry when I get like this.

So yes, I suppose I thought I was ironing. I certainly didn't feel any pain, not until far later. That's the terrible thing about burns, the hot sting continues for weeks after the initial incident and only settles when soaked under running water, but I can't spend my life tied to a sink. I thought I was ironing which is why it was such a surprise when I looked down at my hand and saw the iron clamped on top, and realised that horrible smell I'd been noticing had actually been my flesh.

"We must stop demonising men and start healing the rift that feminism has created between men and women."

- Erin Pizzey, social activist, 2020

I can't keep going back to this place. He tells me that they want to heal me, but it hurts. I scream when it happens. I wish I didn't, but the feeling is so horrible, like lightning jabbing into my ears.

I can't remember as well as I used to. Things slip my mind. I swear it's because of the shocks. It's strange. I keep being told that they're meant to save me, and yet every time I go back there, I wish that I was dead.

"I don't want to do this," I say to him.

"Now, honey," he sighs. "Don't make this difficult. You know they're only halfway through your treatment."

I try a different tactic, one that's prone to success.

"Darling." I place my hand on his thigh while he's driving, scoot round in the seat so that I'm leaning towards him. "Let's not today, huh? I'm feeling so much better. Honestly, I am. Let's go and get an ice-cream, hey? Now, that'll really make me feel calm, a nice vanilla cone, maybe a walk by the seaside."

He smiles.

"After, honey, after."

I shriek in frustration, slam my hand down on the leather seat.

"I can't *eat* after. You know I can't. My jaw is too tight, and I just want to... I just want to..."

"Rest?" He looks at me. "See, look how het up you are. *This* is why we're doing this honey, because look at you. Do you think this is healthy?" He shakes his head again, and I feel more insulted than relieved that there's a clear flicker of sympathy. "This is for your own good."

I sulk for the rest of the journey, but I'm not going to get anywhere with him when he's this determined. Anything I say to the contrary will just make it worse. But when we pull up on that gravel path and the hospital is right ahead of me with its wide, black doors and stone steps, I no longer stay quiet.

"No," I say, shaking my head. "No, I'm not going in. I'm not, I'm not...'

"Now you're being childish."

"I can't," I say, sobbing, a lump rising in my throat. "I can't. I can't do it again. I can't. You won't make me. I can't, I can't..."

My husband leaves the car, and I know he's gone to get the doctors for me. I reach out towards him, try to grab him by the trouser leg:

"No!" I shout, but I miss, and he slams the door and leaves me crying inside. I want to leave, but he has the key. Of course, the doors are locked. "No!" I shout again, sobbing unreservedly now. "No, no, no!" I'm barely conscious of myself doing it, but I start lifting my legs, kicking at the window screen to try and break it. My husband comes back with the doctor now and two other members of staff who don't have white coats. *The muscle*, I think, cynically. I cry harder when he unlocks and opens the car door.

"Baby, no please. I'm begging you."

An orderly lifts me up from under the arms.

"If she continues like this, we may have to consider a treatment more permanent than electro-shock therapy," the doctor tells my husband. I struggle, but it's no use. The two orderlies have such a rough grip on my arm that I can only force myself down to the floor in the hopes they won't move forward, but they just pick me up and drag me by my feet. My shins scrape against the gravel drive, and I know that these people have no intention of keeping me safe.

"Please, don't do this," I cry again, whimpering slightly, but their faces are set. They must deal with this kind of thing every day.

"What kind of treatment do you mean?" my husband asks.

"We've seen a lot of success with the trans-orbital lobotomy."

It takes an embarrassingly short amount of time for them to get me in the chair and before I know it, I'm strapped in. I scream the entire time, which they say will make it worse, but I can't help it.

"It's best to stay calm," they say, but I know from experience that calm doesn't help me any. I scream when they place the gel on my temples and I scream when they strap my head in and I scream even louder when the voltage is high and the electricity is shooting through me like a buzzing needle, and I smell the burning of my grey matter, and I feel so very alive but God, I sure wish that I wasn't.

"It is the mission of A Voice for Men to provide education and encouragement to men and boys; to lift them above the din of misandry, to reject the unhealthy demands of gynocentrism in all its forms, and to promote their mental [...] well-being without compromise or apology."

- Paul Elam, A Voice for Men Mission Statement, 2020.

At first, I found his interruptions helpful. It meant I didn't have to describe too much in depth, and his presumptions were so often correct.

"So, basically you're here to report a sexual assault."

"Yeah." I laughed slightly. "Basically." My hands were knotted together on my knee. It's strange how much of this made me feel like a child again. I had come here before when I was fourteen, scarpering off with a slapped wrist and a red face. "I know it's been a long time," I said. "But I was encouraged to…"

"Encouraged?"

"Yes, my therapist said that for the sake of closure…"

"So, you're doing this because your therapist told you to?"

"Right," I said, stuttering. But that wasn't right. I was doing this for me because *I* wanted to. Because that man from my childhood with creeping hands in piano lessons and a freezer full of ice-pops, that man was still living a good life as a pillar of the community while I'd spent the last decade in hospitals and rehabs, exploring my life on lithium while trying to get a slight grasp on what the fuck I'd done to deserve it all and why it kept on happening. But it was true: my therapist encouraging me to go to the police worked as a kind of permission. I preferred to tell people it was all her idea so that I might escape the nagging feeling that it was my fault and that I have no right to do this now.

"Here's the problem we have," the police officer said, sighing as though I was wasting his time. "Whenever you report this kind of incident so many years later, there's no real evidence. Essentially, it's your word against his."

"But you haven't spoken to him yet," I said.

"Do you have any particular reason to think he'll confess?"

"Well no, of course not, but…"

"Listen, I can only give you my advice, and you can choose whether you want to take it, but these kinds of cases tend to drag on for a long, long time and without any evidence we can't guarantee the result you might be hoping for."

He held his hands up in a surrender position, as though he were the one being attacked.

"But can't you gather evidence? Isn't that what you're supposed to do when there's a crime?"

He laughed. I couldn't believe he laughed. I don't know what I expected, maybe a blanket over my shoulder, a cup of sugary tea, a female police officer with a regional accent telling me how brave I was... It all seemed so naïve, now.

"Darling, if only we had the time and the funding, but this isn't CSI. We can't just tear in and accuse the poor sod of underage sex without evidence."

"I'm telling you it happened," I said, and I could hear my voice rising so I tried to control it. "How is that not evidence? What reason do I have to lie?"

He shrugged.

"It happens. People are angry with their exes, want their bosses sacked. People do things for all sorts of mad reasons that most of us would never understand." He looked down at my notes. "You say that you've been sectioned four times?"

"Yes." I swallowed. He didn't continue and I felt a need to fill the awkward gap. "Psychosis and PTSD... My doctors say it's a result of the sexual abuse. *Extreme* sexual abuse," I added.

I'd learned through many, many group sessions that this wasn't something to be ashamed of, but in front of this officer I felt ashamed. Damaged goods. Too spoilt to bother stitching up or wringing out. He raised his eyebrows but didn't say anything. "Surely, that's evidence?" I asked, my voice cracking. He winced.

"If anything, it's the opposite, love. I'm sorry." He placed his hands flat on the table. "Look, I'm not trying to discourage you from pressing charges, far from it. But it's a very trying process. You'd have to go through this story many times, with a lot of people. You have to withstand questioning... Do you think you'll be stable enough, emotionally, to handle it?"

As though in response, my eyes immediately filled with tears. Had I wanted to say yes, it wouldn't have made a difference. My throat was too constricted. The officer patted my arm, and for a second, I wondered if I'd imagined it all. Had he really been unfair, or was I just particularly sensitive about this kind of thing? Something about the way I acted must have let this neighbour know I was extra vulnerable, that it would be easy for him to get away with it with me. He was right.

Outside, I smoked a cigarette and tried to calm down. My breath was juddery and the long, thick exhales helped, although people gave me evils when they saw me outside lighting up. No doubt they thought I'd been picked up for prostitution or something equally dodgy. Well, it's not like I was above that. I caught a glimpse of my reflection in the shiny, black windows. My roots had grown to my ears and my dye-job had turned my hair wispy and damaged at the ends. My mascara was halfway down my face. To these uptight police officers, I knew what I must look like.

The cigarette was burning between my fingers now, hurting the skin around my nails which had turned pink from having been bitten so often. I should have thrown it on the ground and stamped it out. I should have walked away. Instead, I leant against the handrail, and I watched the filter burn between my fingers. I hadn't hurt myself for quite a long time, but it seemed right, somehow, to put out the smouldering cigarette on the inside of my wrist before I walked away. The pain was a relief, reflective of who I was. It was good, finally, to accept this.

"I challenge you to consider the consequences of those false allegations for the people they are targeting: When we assume the person being accused is guilty before conducting an investigation, or even hold onto that assumption if the outcome of that investigation does not prove their guilt, it can be incredibly damaging to their careers, their reputations, their relationships, and their mental health."

Karlyn Borysenko, *Forbes Magazine*, "The Dark Side Of #MeToo: What Happens When Men Are Falsely Accused," February 2020

Old Soldiers

Teenagers on buses sit in quartets, and I must be getting older because I can't help but worry that one boy is wearing a t-shirt that doesn't seem appropriate for the temperature. It's not freezing, but it's definitely still jacket weather. I used to always be freezing cold on nights out, tiny little dresses, strappy heels, the lot, but not anymore. Now I'm always buttoned up in over-sized jackets, high-necked t-shirts, nothing too revealing, nothing that might get me in trouble. I wish I could say I preferred it.

Everyone else in the gang wears hoodies—a sure sign of delinquency if ever there was one—blasting music through tinny speakers on a Samsung S5. The kind of monotonous beats and squealing electro is intended for no other plat-form than a tinny phone speaker, and potentially no other setting than a bus. No one would listen to this song on a record player in a lounge with solid wood flooring. No one would buy the CD for a family car trip. It seems this music's sole purpose is to antagonise through mild irritation, and judging by the passive aggressive tuts from the other passengers, it's working. Surprisingly, I don't mind it. I quite like the distraction.

I'm using the teenagers as a yardstick to measure where this bus might be heading, but their presence tells me nothing. They could be going to the centre of town, to some street corner near a McDonalds where they can hang about doing nothing and feeling like it's something. It could be to an estate where one of the boys might live with a fairly liberal parent who doesn't mind what they're smoking as long as they do it in the house. I might be being horribly presumptuous. As far as I know, they could be heading to the opera.

I hope we're going to a train station. Better yet, an airport.

The boy's inappropriately un-thermal t-shirt is interesting. I have no idea whether the picture it displays is a generic stock image, but if I had to guess, I would wager it's an album cover, although supposedly not from the artist they're currently choosing to inflict. An old soldier smokes a cigarette, looks right into the camera lens. Old soldiers used to smoke cigarettes, and I wonder how they were able to run away from the bombs so quickly if their chests were tight all the time, and I remember that my chest is tight all the time, and I'm managing to run away without it causing any conceivable problems as of yet. I fancy a cigarette, despite my chest feeling tight, but we're not allowed to smoke inside, so I don't. I wonder if the teenagers have cigarettes. Something tells me they do, but of course, I couldn't ask.

The bell rings. Next stop. A man in tracksuit bottoms and tattered trainers stumbles up the aisle, his hand on the backs of seats then swinging between the yellow, vertical bars. He'll lose his footing when the bus judders to a stop, I just know it, and he does. Still, he thanks the driver before he gets off. The rage I feel towards anyone who doesn't thank a bus driver is unprecedented. I sometimes want them *not* to thank a driver just so that I can experience the intense vitriol, the adrenaline fuelled heart-palpitation which allows me to scoff and mutter "fucking unbelievable" under my breath while I feel a sense of unjust superiority. Anger makes me feel awake, but this man thanked the bus driver, so I don't feel anything. I just look out of the window, and I try not to think about how much I want a cigarette.

I kick my suitcase, which isn't really a suitcase. It's big enough to run away with but nowhere near large enough to constitute as a suitcase, and besides, it has no wheels. I call it a suitcase because I liked the idea of packing my bags and going, wheeling along the pavement in a trench coat and sunglasses, but in the end, there wasn't time. It's funny. The things you pack should be the things you use the most, and yet they're hardly ever the things you actually need. Old soldiers would have a better chance of escaping bombs the less they were carrying. Although they certainly would have had to carry something. No one can come in completely defenceless against a shedload of artillery; they'd be absolutely fucked. I am realising, as I look down at my not-quite suitcase, that I am absolutely fucked.

There's an old man on the bus who looks old enough to have been in war, maybe old enough to have posed for a picture just like the one on the teenagers' inappropriately un-thermal t-shirt. Maybe not the *World* War, but *a* war at the very least. Maybe one of the Asian ones: Korea, Malaysia, Vietnam, something of that ilk. I know very little about wars. I seem to think that all of those were around the same time, somewhere between the forties and the seventies, but maybe I should research more. The only thing that I remember distinctly from weird, moustachioed, greasy kids in the playground is the Japanese torture method where they tied people to bamboo plants and let the stick grow through them, knowing that the seeds grew outrageously quickly. Outstandingly strong stuff, bamboo. It can pierce through skin and organs, although presumably not bone. I check the older man for any sign he's been kebabed in the past, but no. He seems relatively healthy for his age. He has a face which droops down, but his eyes seem bright. I always think that people with bright eyes can't be traumatised. Conversely, children with bloodshot eyes *terrify* me.

I check the teenagers to see if their eyes are bloodshot, but I can't really tell. I know that my eyes don't shine nicely anymore, but I'm not quite traumatised. I'm definitely not traumatised enough to compare myself to a soldier. That would be bordering on offensive. I've never even seen a bamboo plant, although as a woman I understand the agony of a penetrating stick. I want to ask the old man if he's ever been in any war and if it was in Asia, and if he smoked while he was running, and if he had a cigarette now, but you can't smoke inside, and anyway he's ringing the bell and he's stumbling up and I wouldn't have the time to ask him before he departs, so I don't.

The bus judders still. He nearly falls but doesn't. I wonder if he'll thank the driver. He does. Another chance for justifiable anger denied. I feel nothing emotionally, but physically my chest feels tight. I shouldn't crave cigarettes when my chest feels tight, but I do. I'll regret it when I have to run away, and again I remind myself that I'm running away right now and my chest does feel tight and I'm still managing fine, and the bus is pulling in, and I recognise the sign that indicates we're at a station and I think that this is it now, this is my chance, and I watch the teenagers to establish what they're doing and, sure enough, the quartet stand, taking their time as they seem to have to wind up headphone wires (which makes no sense to me because they were quite happy to play their music aloud), and they stumble off towards the station, and I notice that one of them, the one with the soldier on his t-shirt, has a rolled-up cigarette behind his ear, and he is likely to be smoking it outside the station before they get their train, and I know how to roll cigarettes from my old university days, so I'm sure he would be happy to lend me one, and I wonder where they're going, and for the first time, I realise that they have luggage, which is partially why they're taking so long to gather up their things, and it occurs to me that this station has a direct link to the airport, and when they leave, three of them thank the driver:

"Cheers!"

"Thanks, pal!"

"Thanks!"

But one of them doesn't, and I want to be angry, but I'm not because I feel like three out of four isn't bad, and they probably assumed that the driver understood their gratitude by this point, so I have finally gotten what I wanted. Someone didn't thank the driver. I still feel nothing, although my chest is tight, and the doors close, and it's too late for me to stumble forward, so I wait, and I think I'll see where this bus ends up, but it turns out, as I pretend not to know (although I really knew all along) that this route is cyclical, and I can't run away from anything. I eventually get off just because I need a cigarette, and I feel slightly safer in this spot as I recognise the street. When I get off the bus, I do not thank the driver. Instead, I stand in the cold, and I breathe and I breathe and I realise that I am exactly where I was at the beginning. I pick up the bag. I find Maggie outside my local with her usual entourage, always out, big gossip, and I pinch a cigarette from her. She asks about the suitcase that isn't really a suitcase. I tell her that I'm not going away, no; I'm just coming back actually. I know it was a mistake to tell her that. For a start, it isn't true, and I've always considered myself an honest person, although recently, out of necessity, that has started to change. If they mention to him that I've been away, and I'm sure they will, there will undoubtedly be an explosion. But then when isn't there an explosion?

I thank Mags for a cigarette. I finish it in a few, long drags, and it doesn't help me breathe any easier but that hardly matters. It doesn't matter if your chest is tight all the time when you opt to run towards the bombs now, does it?

The Original Story of Kerosene Girl

Preached to women internationally is the undeniably sound advice that when attacked by a stranger it is far more effective to shout "fire" than it is to shout the truth. Most innocent bystanders do not want to interfere with the truth.

This was the experience of Kerosene Girl, who at the time went by a different name. Naturally, we cannot be sure if the legend is true. Certain scholars argue for the existence of multiple kerosene girls who have, over time, blurred into one cautionary tale (although what they believe the story is attempting to caution remains unclear). The longevity of Kerosene Girl has many believing that the story stems from medieval folklore, a spin-off from the witch trials, another typical tale of human barbarity. Most historians, however, agree that the events leading up to the death of Kerosene Girl happened much more recently than its status would suggest, around the 1960s. Attempts to measure this accurately prove problematic as the story was passed along through word-of-mouth alone.

What we can fairly predict is that Kerosene Girl was around nine or ten at the time of the event. She'd been sent by her father to the corner shop to pick up more fuel for their barbecue. It was an unseasonably scorching day in April, too hot to be comfortable sitting indoors, and as it was a Saturday and the family didn't have any plans, it was decided that they would all sit outside eating grilled sausages and drinking fizzy pop while the children kicked around a ball on their small expanse of grass. Unfortunately, the barbecue wouldn't stay lit long enough to cook anything, and so the father made the executive decision to send his youngest daughter out in search of fuel.

The owner of the corner shop bashfully informed Kerosene Girl that they didn't sell lighter fluid, and that she must therefore go farther into town where a nice man at the DIY store would be able to help her. He drew a map on the back of an envelope and sent her on her way.

Forever in the spirit of hard-work and competence, Kerosene Girl found the store, explained what she was after, and purchased what was required. She slipped the change into her dungarees' pocket so that she might buy sweeties later if her father neglected to ask for it back (as he often did).

Unfortunately for Kerosene Girl, a strange man had been watching her. He'd seen her examining the envelope and was aware that she must be lost or at the very least far from home. He waited until she was out of the shop and back onto her old country lane, and then he dragged her into an alley between two houses, his hand clamped over her mouth so that she couldn't scream.

Now, Kerosene Girl didn't know what it was that she needed to fear about strange men, but she knew without doubt that she should fear them. Her mother and father had taught her that much, but her *sister* had taught her far more. Her sister had warned her that strange men like beauty, and this she knew well because she was far prettier than Kerosene Girl. Her sister had full lips and olive, clear skin, thick hair piled on top her head like a tower. At least, that's what she looked like in some versions of the story. In other versions, the sister had blonde hair and blue eyes, standing as thin as a rake with a smile like mischief. In other versions, she was curvy well beyond her years with a heaving bust and ample bottom, a waist you could squeeze perfectly between two hands. Sometimes she spoke Spanish, sometimes French or Swahili. Sometimes she smoked cigarettes, sometimes she peeled fruit with perfect, pointed fingernails, but the one thing we understand to be a historical certainty is that she was very, very beautiful.

Now, Kerosene Girl wasn't quite as astounding as her sister was, but a whisper of beauty still shone out in her features. This gave her older sister cause for alarm. She taught Kerosene Girl that when a strange man grabs you, you act like a beast. You scream and you shriek and you roar like a lion. You speak out in tongues and you laugh maniacally. You fight, you scratch, you bite, you kick, and you aim all of this *down there*. Bizarre behaviours will turn a strange man away. If all else fails and you find you can't defend yourself, remember to shout "fire," as that way people are more likely to intervene.

Kerosene Girl was bright in all senses, and she remembered her sister's advice. She kicked, she screamed, she weed her knickers, and all the while she shouted: *FIRE, FIRE, FIRE!* She splashed the kerosene around hoping that people might believe her if they smelled gas, splashing herself and the strange man and the brick wall and concrete floor surrounding her. She bit the hand over her mouth every time he tried to silence her and insisted on causing a fuss. But the strange man just smiled. He was maddeningly unphased.

"Little girl," he said sadly, almost sweetly, "what are you hoping to achieve? Do you think you can escape this? You might be able to *this* time, but if it's not me now, it'll be someone else later. Why do you think all you pretty, little girls know how to do this? And ask yourself, does it change anything?"

Kerosene Girl remembered her older sister's eyes. She'd seen eyes like that everywhere, tainted with that mixture of shame and silence, of damage best forgotten, of hope that it might not be too late to save someone else. Kerosene Girl understood then that there was never a chance. She was born unsalvageable.

She nodded to the man, understanding that it would be easier if she was complicit. She held out her hand to him and he grabbed it. In her other hand, she held onto the kerosene. It was still important to her that she didn't let her father down. They exited the ginnel, no longer afraid of being seen in public. The strange man didn't worry about her acting out anymore.

Unfortunately for the strange man, he happened to walk past a young gentleman in a waistcoat and a curled moustache, with a beautifully whimsical and frankly, outdated, tobacco pipe. The young gentleman nodded brightly at the two of them, twirling his moustache before he lit the match.

Now of course, this youngster couldn't be to blame. He didn't know that both the strange man and Kerosene Girl were coated in lighter fluid. Still, up they went in a ball of flames. The strange man jumped up and down, attempting to take off his jacket as the fire continued to spread up the sleeve. Eventually he remembered to stop, drop, and roll, and a small crowd began to gather, rushing outside as they saw, and smelt, the spectacle. People ran to grab their hoses, but the village was in a drought, and it was hard for them to get the water necessary to help put out the strange man.

Kerosene Girl had already badly burned her hands and her clothes were smoking. She could smell the singeing of her hair. She walked slowly to the middle of the road and sat say. People gathered around her, wafting pathetically, unsure of what to do. She remembered what the strange man had said to her, and she understood the truth behind his words. It was sad, but in this way, she knew she could still beat him. She could leave the world unscathed. So, Kerosene Girl poured the rest of the gasoline over herself.

She sat in the road, calm and resolute, no longer shouting madly in tongues, no longer screaming "fire." She sat and burned and felt a sense of pride in her complete self-sacrifice. It was the only way, one must suppose, she could manage to maintain some control with regard to her future. The strange man recovered from his minor injuries after a brief trip to A&E and some major aquatic dousing.

Of course, part of the mystery shrouding Kerosene Girl is that when her body was recovered, there was no way of identifying her due to the extremity of her injuries. Then, of course, there's the argument that Kerosene Girl was a figure of fantasy long before the story from the 1960s emerged, and that this therefore indisputably proves that our writer's particular depiction of events is "inaccurate to the point of self-indulgent projection" as one critic so tactfully claimed. Still, there's no denying that Kerosene Girl lives on in our hearts as she smoulders on a million pavements, in a million countries, over a million historical moments. Again, it's hard to tell why she's considered to be a cautionary tale. I personally see nothing the girl did wrong.

Proud Boy

Proud Boy was born to a mother who loved him terribly and a father who didn't dare cry in the delivery room. Proud Boy had nightmares about monsters under the bed. Proud Boy would sneak under the covers in his parents' room until his father told him off for being soft. Proud Boy didn't have any brothers or sisters, and his kindergarten teacher said that Proud Boy really ought to learn how to share. Proud Boy was very bright for his age. Proud Boy learned how to read and write with ease, but Proud Boy had to sit very close to the front. Proud Boy needed glasses to see the board, which his father said made him look like a nerd. Proud Boy realised he had outgrown his father intellectually.

Proud Boy started middle school. Proud Boy noticed girls. Proud Boy liked girls with freckles and sticky lip-gloss and hair tied in braids and ponytails. Proud Boy also liked girls with big breasts and big asses who wore too much makeup and laughed at bad jokes. Proud Boy knew he was too smart for them, and after listening to them speak for too long with idiot boys who couldn't hold a conversation, he started to hate these girls, even if his dick would disagree. When Proud Boy started to masturbate, he watched pretty girls with mascara streaking down their cheeks while they were fucked. Proud Boy spent a lot of time on his computer.

Proud Boy's grades started to slip. Proud Boy wasn't the cleverest anymore. Proud Boy's essays got low grades because he said things the teacher claimed were historically inaccurate. Proud Boy knew that what he wrote was true. Proud Boy had checked the facts online. Proud Boy thought that people were trying to silence the real truth, and that most idiots were too conformist not to question this authoritarian state. Proud Boy was a lot smarter than they gave him credit for. Proud Boy's history teacher wrote a note home suggesting that his parents limit his internet usage.

Proud Boy stopped doing well in English. Proud Boy hated reading books that told him he was bad just because he was both Proud and Boy. Proud Boy didn't think racism existed anymore. Proud Boy knew for a fact that girls had it easier because they didn't have to fight in wars, and they never had to get real jobs like emptying out trash cans or going down the mines. Proud Boy thought that people should let go of the past and stop being so pathetic about it. Proud Boy had never done anything wrong. Why was Proud Boy getting the blame?

Proud Boy talked to other boys online who told him he was ugly. Proud Boy was small for his age and a little too thick round the middle. Proud Boy stopped wearing his glasses, so he didn't look like so much like a nerd. Proud Boy started to get a lot of headaches. Proud Boy didn't get sex. Proud Boy thought girls were shallow. Proud Boy was told that girls would cheat on you if they wanted to and lie about rape to get money and power. Proud Boy watched a lot of videos of girls with fists inside them, tied up against uncomfortable looking machinery, and Proud Boy found it funny.

Proud Boy's parents got a divorce. Proud Boy's mother says she needed to find herself. Proud Boy's mother went to a temple in India in order to speak with god. She wanted to experience humility and deeper spiritual truth surrounded by the haze of incense smoke and bullshit. Proud Boy stayed at home with his father. Proud Boy's father drank a lot. Proud Boy and his father didn't talk. Proud Boy and his father watched a lot of TV shows where there were laughter tracks, but neither of them laughed. Proud Boy went online and told his friends that his mother was a slut. Proud Boy's friends agreed. They photoshopped her picture onto a naked woman with the word splayed across her chest in cherry-red lipstick, her breasts tied up like bags of purple sand. Proud Boy forced himself to laugh.

Proud Boy got in a fight at school. Proud Boy thought Sad Girl was fucking stupid. Sad Girl was crying because her brother had gotten arrested. Sad Girl told her friends that they couldn't afford the bail. Sad Girl said that when they took him, his face was all bloody. That scared Sad Girl. Sad Girl didn't want him to die in prison. Proud Boy said that maybe her brother should have complied. Proud Boy said that everyone knew that her brother sold drugs. Proud Boy said the police were doing their job getting scum like that off the street. Sad Girl told him to go to hell. Later, Sad Girl's younger brother (two grades below Proud Boy) punched Proud Boy in the face. People said Sad Girl's little brother was a legend. Sad Girl's little brother got suspended and his mother dragged him out of school by his ear, looking angry and very, very tired. Proud Boy didn't fight back. Proud Boy thought it was telling that these fucking monkeys were too stupid to argue back with words. Proud Boy was the smartest boy in school. Proud Boy was gonna be a philosopher. Proud Boy was gonna be a billionaire. Proud Boy shared a video of a B.B.C. gangbang and told everyone it was Sad Girl at a family reunion. Proud Boy's friends told him he was funny.

Proud Boy cared about logic, not feelings. Proud Boy knew how to take responsibility for himself. Proud Boy knew you couldn't rely on anyone. Proud Boy learned you had to be ready to fight back. Proud Boy was a renegade. Proud Boy was a freedom fighter. Proud Boy was a lone wolf. Proud Boy wasn't scared of anything. Proud Boy didn't conform to society's fucked-up norms.

When Proud Boy reached high school, he was not well liked. Proud Boy didn't sleep a lot. Proud Boy didn't shower. Proud Boy played a lot of video games. Proud Boy hated gamer girls with their stupid knee-high socks and pink hair, taking selfies while they slobbered all over a controller. Proud Boy said that he hoped they all got raped. Proud Boy fucking meant it.

Proud Boy found his people. Proud Boy had a gang. Proud Boy's mother came back from her trip and moved in with her new friend Prishi. Proud Boy told her to go fuck herself. Proud Boy's mother gave him money to put into his "college fund." Proud Boy took it out and bought an AK47. Proud Boy found it easy. The man who owned the store said that he liked Proud Boys like Proud Boy. Proud Boy knew exactly what he meant.

Proud Boy saw videos online of people in bala-clavas throwing soup cans and bricks. Proud Boy thought they should be set on fire. Proud Boy saw a car mow down a bunch of snowflakes and he laughed. Proud Boy couldn't wait to get a licence.

Proud Boy saw the president, all suited up and kicking ass. Proud Boy liked the idea that he was getting his home back, his land, his America where he would be a king. Proud Boy wanted things to go back to the way they'd been before. Proud Boy wanted appreciation. Proud Boy wanted respect.

Proud Boy stood down.

Proud Boy stood by.

Well, what the fuck do you think's gonna happen?

Centurion

It wasn't so much a shower of confetti as a pathetic ejaculation. Party poppers always have more bark than bite, and while the weak, paper string had very little effect, the deafening crackles made Phyllis flinch. Her offspring were wearing plastic, gladiator helmets, red feathers sticking up from the middle as with cockerels. *That's what they all look like,* she thought. *Cocks.* Bobby had decked himself out in full toga, showing off his pasty chest and spotty arms.

Dorothy, Phyllis' daughter who insisted on being called "Dotty," as though the world was too dim to handle polysyllabic names, had popped round last weekend on her usual post-church irritation mission.

"Mum, you know it's your birthday next week? Do you remember how old you are?"

Phyllis had discovered in the past twenty years or so that she needn't respond to anything if she didn't feel like it.

"You're going to be 100! Isn't that exciting? You'll get a letter from the Queen. You'll be a Centurion, like the old Romans."

Phyllis knew that wasn't the right word, but as she couldn't remember what the right word was, she let it go. The quieter she managed to remain, the quicker the visits usually went.

"Bobby and Michelle were saying we could have a party. Won't that be nice? We can bring sandwiches and tea. And cake, of course. Bobby even thought," and here she paused to laugh at something Phyllis was certain would incense her, "we could do a little Centurion theme, you know? All dressed up as Romans? And Michelle can bring the grandbabies. What do you think?"

Phyllis couldn't envision anything worse. The idea of spending hours with those pre-pubescent brats made her skin crawl. Thankfully, Phyllis knew she wouldn't live to see the day. Every morning, she'd been waking up so tired that her bones ached. She couldn't use her legs at all now, relying solely on her chair. She carted around intravenous machines more often than she didn't, and since her throat operation thirty years ago, she spoke exclusively through an electronic device embedded in her neck. Supposedly, this was meant to be a warning against smoking, but Phyllis didn't regret a single cigarette. In fact, she wished she'd smoked more so that cancer might have taken her earlier than the care-home had. Her Robert had the good grace to go early. That was the way to do it.

"Whatever you like," Phyllis' machine said for her. Dorothy was pleased. Phyllis comforted herself with the thought that at least they'd already be gathered for the funeral.

To her ever-lasting disappointment, however, Phyllis kept waking up. Every morning, she would awake to darkness, clenching her eyelids shut and willing them not to flicker open, but they always did. Since the universe was proving too incompetent, she decided to take matters into her own hands. The nurses (all barely out of school with hoop-earrings and terribly common accents) took extra care when washing Phyllis' face due to the electro-larynx. As luck would have it, the morning before the party, a young and inexperienced carer had the privilege of bathing her. She spent many long minutes chattering away about her boyfriend's tattoos, exacerbating Phyllis' suicidal ideation.

"And he wants his neck done now, but I'm like, what about jobs, babe?"

"I have new soap," Phyllis' robot voice shrieked for her. "Bedside table. Lavender. Birthday present."

"Oh! How nice. I'll fetch it for you, pet."

The carer toddled off. Wasting very little time, Phyllis submerged herself under the water. She understood the laws of electricity and respected that it would be a merciful death, but failing that, drowning was always an option. The new carer wasn't bright, and seeing as the soap didn't exist (no one ever got Phyllis presents she actually

117

liked), she could be gone for hours. Alas, it wasn't meant to be. Ms. Usman, the only carer with any medical competency, grabbed her out of the water well before any damage could be done.

"Oh, sugar! Mrs. Wayne, can you hear me?" she shouted in her thumping Nigerian accent. Phyllis intended to inform her, calmly, that she had been trying to die. She was therefore perturbed to find that she couldn't speak. The electro-larynx had been completely frazzled.

No matter. The party could continue as planned provided a notebook and pen were provided to serve as her voice. Phyllis only wished that she could scream in frustration.

Bobby knelt down in front of her, smiling pityingly as his head tilted to the side.

"Grandma," he said slowly. He picked up her hand and brought it to his lips before placing it gently on his cheek. If Phyllis had the strength, she would have slapped him. "I'm in awe of your longevity. The things you must have seen. The history…"

And nothing can be worse than your dreadlocks, she thought, bringing a smile unwittingly to her face.

"I would be honoured if you could share just one asset of your wisdom with me." He held out the pen for her to take.

With shaking fingers, Phyllis flipped through the notebook, looking for the only page on which she'd been able to write anything. Bobby leaned forward in anticipation.

"What is it, Mum?" Dorothy added, her hand resting on her son's bare shoulder. Phyllis found the page in which the one, singular word was written:

"ARTHRITIS," it said. She pointed at it, then dropped the pen on the floor, watching it roll away across the wooden panelling onto the gravel.

"Oh, Mum," Dorothy sighed.

"No, no, it's fine. I understand. I can see everything I want to know in those wise, old eyes," Bobby said. Phyllis tried to make her eyes tell him to get fucked.

"Here Rosco, go take your great-gran some cake," Michelle said.

Well, if Phyllis had a problem with Bobby's revealing attire, Michelle's was something else. Three children and breasts lurched up so high they could poke an eye out. No wonder her son was such a stupid dunderwhelp. Her mouth would hang open too if that's what her mother wore to a family do.

Rosco placed the cake on her lap wordlessly. It was all cream and jam, sticky sponge that seemed, frankly, under-baked. There was no chance Phyllis was going to manage it with her teeth.

"Made it myself, Nan," Michelle called over.

Ah well. No matter. It would be inedible anyway. Phyllis placed it carefully on the tray table.

"Isn't it nice to have the party in the garden?" Dorothy asked, spreading her arms wide. "I tell you what, I'd love to have my birthday in the summer."

"Well, all the seasons have their own certain *je ne sais quoi*," Bobby added.

"Shall we do cards and pressies?" Michelle said with a clap of her hands. "My boys have something special for you!"

The three of them (all different hues, Phyllis couldn't help but notice, and the first one born when she was just sixteen!) rushed over. The two younger ones, called Kayden and Zaiden or some such nonsense, fought over who would give it to her while Rosco stood with his usual gormlessness. They plopped it on her lap. Phyllis stared at it with disdain.

"Let me help you with the paper, Mum," Dorothy added, reaching over to gently undo the bow. Little by little, the gift came into view and Phyllis still had no clue what it was she was looking at.

"It's a pen holder!" Michelle said. "Rosco made it at school, and we all helped paint it."

Dorothy and Bobby ooohed and aaaahed in recognition. Phyllis rolled her eyes. It was a lump of rock coated in sparkles and mismatching colours.

"That's lovely, pet," Dorothy said.

"Well, they inherited my artistic talent." Michelle smiled. "Int that nice, Gran?" Michelle shouted down to her. "You can put in all your pens."

Phyllis shook the notebook back at her: *ARTHRITIS.*

"Now, I don't claim to be as talented as these lads of yours," Bobby said, "but my present is a little bit on the creative side, too."

This time it was the women who ooohed in surprise as Bobby pulled a guitar from around the corner of the French doors leading into the reception area, unzipping it carefully from its pristine case. Phyllis felt dread grip her.

"This is a song I wrote for you, Grandma, on your birthday. It's called Centurion."

That's not the right word, Phyllis thought again as he settled himself into a comfortable A minor chord.

If ever anyone has to describe hell, they'll most likely describe something "hot." Fire and brimstone. Eternal damnation. When Phyllis was younger, she and Robert would spend her birthday in bed under a single layer of sheets. It would only be at the night-time when it was cooler and far more pleasant that they would wander along the promenades and beaches, stopping off at cocktail bars to drink more than was decent and dance along to all their silly songs. That was music, the kind that makes you kiss under the stars and want to spin around in exaltation, the beauty of piano and trumpets. Jazz crackled under your skin and seeped into your heart, making it beat twice as quickly. Not like this fucking caterwauling. Phyllis' hell was hot and full of shrieks as Bobby yelped out melodies (although melodies was perhaps a grandiose term) and then, dear god, when it couldn't possibly get any worse, the boy started to rap:

"Yo Granny P

It's your birth D!"

And Michelle laughed along delightedly, failing to hide her cringing expression.

"Yeah!" she shouted, raising her hand.

It seemed like the delusional embarrassment was coming to an end, and the song would be, if not good at the very least over, but it wasn't. He slowed down. One strum for each chord. He tried to warble the lyrics like he was some sort of pop-star (Phyllis wondered why there were no singers these days who knew how to hold a bloody note) and sang slowly and deliberately.

"'Cause you're a Centurion…"

Everyone clapped and cheered.

"Aww, that was lovely, Bobby," Michelle said condescendingly, and Dorothy (Phyllis always knew, ever since her birth, that there was something wrong with that child) wiped away a tear from her eyes.

"That was beautiful."

"Well, it's good actually because I wrote it for Gran, but I managed to play it to Ezra at his funeral, so that was meaningful, too," Bobby added.

"Aw, pet, I know you miss him."

"Well, he's in a better place now," Bobby said, smiling melancholically. "And he was a Centurion too! Lived to 100!"

"Cats don't live that long," Zaiden or Kayden said.

"Ah, but for every human year, that's four cat years, don't you know?" Bobby said. "So technically, Ezra was 100 when he died."

Technically, Phyllis wanted to argue, the cat had been dead for years. What kind of evil creature allows a cat to live to twenty-five years of age? It was only a ball of meat and fur by the end of its life, thin as a rake with a long flapping belly, smelling of shit and the various ointments that Bobby rubbed into its skin (visible through the fur). That was when Phyllis had last seen it in person, but Bobby still kept it for *years* after that. He personalised his Christmas cards with pictures of this poor, sick, corpse of creature, when there'd have been more mercy in a harsh whack with a shovel. It had died from an infection, shit dropping down the back of its legs for the maggots to crawl over.

Phyllis didn't want to go like that. She hoped that they would have the mercy to let her go with grace, but no. Like everyone else in her cruel, little genetic circle, they forced her into old age with no dignity, left her gasping as nurses yanked her out of lukewarm water before parading in front of her in ridiculous costumes like a play that felt as though it had no end (*or so*, Phyllis thought on reflection, *like a play*).

Her saviour, Ms. Usman, the only competent carer, popped out through the French doors into the garden.

"Hello, everyone. Mrs. Wayne, can I get anything for you?" Phyllis stared at her with wide and desperate eyes. "Are we getting a little tired?" she asked, and Phyllis nodded quickly.

"Aw, alright, well it was lovely seeing you, Mum," Dorothy said, planting a sloppy kiss on her cheek.

"And I'll see you later, Grandma." Bobby pulled her in the opposite direction, his sweaty armpit round her neck.

"Say bye to your gran, you lot," Michelle commanded, followed by a depressing round of grunts and groans in the vague area of a proper goodbye from her entourage. Ms. Usman went to wheel Phyllis back in, but first, Phyllis raised her hand. She picked up the notebook. Her family leaned forward in excitement.

"What is it, Mrs, Wayne?" the nurse asked.

"Is there something you want to say to us, Mum?"

The thought did cross her mind that she could beg for death. She worried that it may fall on willfully deaf ears. She had exaggerated her arthritis, but it did hurt her to write and she didn't want to get into a philosophical debate on the Shakespearean right *to not be*. Phyllis supposed, from the stupid grins of their faces, that they thought she was going to thank them. She wasn't. It suddenly came to her exactly what it was that she needed to say.

It's Centenarian, she wrote. It had finally come to her. She dropped the pen back on the wooden panelling, refusing to use that nonsense disguised at a penholder, and watched it roll all the way onto the grass. As she was wheeled back into her room, she could vaguely see in the reflection of the French doors her families' faces collectively resting in the shared disappointment of an anti-climax.

You Mean
Everything

I found the earrings on the bedside table. Not boxed up or new. Not mine—of course not mine, there'd be no story here—and I knew that my relationship was irreparably damaged. It was like looking at a young body, firm muscle and slim frame, smooth flesh in all the perfect places, a genuine rhapsodic masterpiece, right before an X-ray scanned over it all with an ugly flash of blue and showed me that actually, the bones were all horrifically broken underneath. [REDACTED] had been unfaithful. This would prove to be a massive inconvenience.

I wasn't speaking to my friends as often, not because he'd told me I couldn't, just because it was awkward. I knew they didn't like him. I justified it as growing maturity on my part. My friends seemed jealous that I'd slipped into an adult situation so quickly when they were still going out clubbing, something I'd never really enjoyed even when I was single. Anyway, I found new friends in our co-workers. I'd believed their kind, sympathetic glances meant they liked me, but now I understood they were looks of pity. They must have known that he was having an affair. Everyone must have known.

I didn't know who it was he was sleeping with, but it hardly mattered. Had it been a man I loved, I would have been desperately jealous. I would have stalked through pages and pages of social media, analysing every like and comment. I would have held the earrings under a zoomed-in camera to see if I could find the tiniest of hairs that might give away a clue, but as it was, the actual woman was meaningless to me. It was probably the new receptionist. Isn't it always? Anyway, he'd flirted with her at the Halloween party.

The theme had been 80s hits. I'd wanted to go as Cyndi Lauper, proud as I was of my natural gingerness, but [REDACTED], in a rare show of foresight and organisation, had made me a costume in advance. He thought it was the funniest idea he'd ever had, so I donned the plain black t-shirt he'd had customised with one of those plastic-y white slogans reading: "I'm Eileen." The novelty of the pun lasted no longer than the walk into the pub, but the smell of toothpaste and yoghurt lingered all night. [REDACTED] got steadily drunker and flirted with the receptionist, who looked thrillingly sexy as a pointy-bra'd Madonna. He'd dressed in a leather vest and latex trousers, a gorgeous Alice Cooper in his black lipstick and scruffy wig. All the trips to the gym had been worth it. His arms were toned and strong, and as he leant against the bar, I could see a thin line where muscle met flesh. I didn't feel turned on, though. I hadn't been turned on in a while, but that wasn't because I didn't like the look of him, more because I didn't like the look of myself.

I'd had to catch my breath in the toilet cubical. **[REDACTED]** was always the life of the party. I was the tag-along that people pulled nice faces at. I washed my hands and glanced at myself in the bumpy bathroom mirror. My mascara had rubbed under my eyes, and I was getting spots on my chin. Worse than that, my hair was limp, and I looked fat. In my oversized, toothpaste-y t-shirt, I looked like I was heading for bed rather than a glamourous costume party. It was mortifying.

Perhaps the receptionist would have looked good as Eileen. Perhaps, instead of being sour-faced and insecure all night, she'd have looked fun and boyish. One of the lads. She'd make crude comments and the office would have laughed in surprise. (Such filth coming out of a *girl*? Surely not!)

I could never be that person. I was serious to the point of bordering on wet. I couldn't take a joke. I'd spent my Master's degree picking apart verses of poetry and searching for hidden meaning behind a line break or a change of rhythm, losing myself in the synesthetic connection between the sounds and the sensations, small tingles behind my ears. **[REDACTED]** had always rolled his eyes when I spoke about it. He said it was pretentious, and I suppose it was. When I started seeing him and introduced him to my friends, I flinched whenever any of them used a polysyllabic word or referred to anything as "derivative" or "compelling." **[REDACTED]** was very much of the attitude that the curtains were fucking blue.

I'd dropped so many of my characteristics in order to be attractive to him, that the further the relationship developed, the more it felt immoral to slip back into my actual personality. I could have left after the third date when I heard his transphobic comments, but I thought that to expect perfect social understanding was middle-class snobbishness. I could have left when he said that Meghan Markel was playing the race card, when he'd argued that girls who tricked men with too much makeup were just as bad as men who secretly removed condoms. Instead, I justified that debate was healthy, that without someone to challenge me, I'd be stuck in an echo chamber with no understanding of how the world worked or what normal people felt. I used to believe that there would be people who'd love me the way I was, but the more I looked around as a heterosexual woman, the more I realised that wasn't true. The few left-wing men I knew were flooded with so many options, it was easier for them to find someone pretty and quiet that they could treat them with respect just as easily as they could an angry, orange-haired feminist.

Again, that zap, that bright blue shock. I thought about the changes I'd undergone in the name of what I had disingenuously dubbed self-improvement. I worked on my anger issues. I tried to be less uptight and pretentious. I didn't bring up my degree anymore. Stuck as I was in an admin assistant role in the same company where everyone else had a handful of GCSEs, the pride I held in my intelligence came across as arrogance, which of course it was. I had to let it go and learn to laugh. Funnily enough though, I can't remember ever having problems laughing before **[REDACTED]** came into my life.

I couldn't go back and analyse everything in our relationship now. My behaviour was so pitiful that flicking back through the memories was painful, more painful than the affair even. I decided instead to play it, fittingly, by ear.

People always hate winter after Christmas, but I don't. There's something communal in the drudgery. I don't mind coming into the office as much because it's not like there's anything outside I'm missing out on. No one minds the extra coffee breaks or the space heater being on full blast. Everyone's off the drink in their dry January attempts, which means **[REDACTED]** doesn't snore and I sleep better. With every open door, you know there's someone entering a room who's glad to be out of the cold, who's going to rub their hands together and say something like:

"God, it's Baltic out there," and I can smile sympathetically and say something normal back. Something like:

"They say it's going to snow next week!"

And then they'll roll their eyes and say:

"Great! That'll be the whole country at a standstill then."

It was the only time of year where the rest of the world was working at the same pace as me, and I could stay in with a takeaway without feeling like a boring bitch who was missing out on all the fun.

I'd worn the mystery earrings since I'd found them. **[REDACTED]** hadn't noticed. I don't know why he would. They were plain, silver hoops, so it wouldn't be as though he'd know that they weren't mine. Innocuous. That was the word. Probably why he'd left them on the bedside table without thinking.

That morning, I was awake before him. I'd been up at 6am, rising with the lazy sun. I stared at him for a while taking it all in: his open mouth, his stubble, the way his chest rose and fell with his breath. I thought about the fact that murdering an adulterous partner was cliché, and instead I got up to shower.

They didn't really need me to do my job, but they kept me on to make the coffee and do all the odd jobs no one else wanted to do. Currently,

I was in the process of digitalising all the old records which went back to the 1850s. It was a never-ending task, and I knew I wouldn't finish it, but it was calming and methodical. Sometimes the screen hurt my eyes, so I'd take a few moments away from the computer to shred financial records. That was almost meditative. I'd slide in the paper, trying to judge the exact moment when I would let go and the machine would grip onto the page like a hungry, devouring lover. I'd stop doing that when the intrusive thoughts would tell me to stick my fingers in. Then I went back to the database. It wasn't a tough job, but it was a job that meant I'd been approved for a mortgage at 25. [REDACTED] worked downstairs in IT.

I'd confronted the receptionist after my lunchbreak.

"Hiya love," she said when I opened the door and stepped in from the cold. In her defence, I'm sure she didn't mean to look so unoriginal, with her beehive, her pink lipstick, her overly contoured cheeks. "God, close the door fast; it's Baltic out there," she continued.

Emotionally, I prepared myself to say something like:

"They say it's going to snow next week," but physically I ended up saying:

"You haven't lost a pair of earrings, have you?"

"Earrings?" She touched her ears where a dangly pair of dreamcatchers hung. "No, not me. Have you found some?"

"Yeah, a pair of silver hoops. Don't know who they belong to."

"Girls' toilet?"

"Bedside table," I said. The new receptionist paused in her clicking, her hand still on the mouse, and I could see her face freezing in shock. It was obvious that I had just accused her of something. Her neck was turning red, but that didn't prove anything. It could have been shame *or* indignation. Before she could respond, I slumped past her to my desk and sat down, kicking my shoes off so that I could put my fluffily socked feet near the space heater.

His favourite dinner was Shepherd's pie. I'd made it for our anniversary every year for the six years that we'd been together. Six years and a month or so since he'd got off with me at the Christmas party. I'd been dressed as a sexy angel and he'd commented on how good I looked all scrubbed up, and it had been so long since I'd actually felt attractive that I'd ended up going back to his. I don't know if this was the exact date of our anniversary. It was the date that Facebook popped up, anyway.

This year, I made the Shephard's pie with a meat-free substitute. **[REDACTED]** wouldn't like it. It was slightly embarrassing to think I was dealing with my partner's affair through passive aggression rather than direct action. I could have filled his pie up with rodenticide, but instead I chose Quorn. Baby steps, I suppose.

We hadn't had sex since I found the earrings, and I thought that would drive him crazy, but he didn't seem to notice. Slightly embarrassing. I'd thought that if I left him without, he'd be on his knees begging, but no. We just went to bed earlier. Perhaps it was the January blues.

I was wearing the earrings, obviously. It felt strange not to wear them now. I found myself playing with them when I was thinking, twisting them round and round through my fingers. I kept them on in the shower even. I started to rely on them for comfort more than I relied on coffee. He still hadn't noticed.

Another thing I did was visit the hairdresser. I got her to shave both sides of my head, just a tiny little bit, just so the ears were all the more visible and I had a boxlike shape to my fringe. It was all the style these days, apparently. She didn't even flinch when I showed her the picture.

"It'll look nice with this colour," she'd said.

"It's nice that I have red hair, isn't it?" I responded. My hair hadn't been complimented in such a long time and it used to be my finest feature. I knew that asking for a compliment so blatantly wasn't good or normal, but I wanted to be positive about something for a change.

"Oh, a hundred percent!" she'd said. "Especially with your freckles, it's adorable."

[REDACTED] didn't like it very much. He scrunched up his nose when he saw it and said it made me look a bit like a lesbian. I had actually experimented with women in college. Everyone who studied poetry did; it was par for the course. Actually, it was one of the only times I'd ever been able to cum. The woman was an insatiable butch who loved my wide-eyed nervousness and was happy to go down on me for the longest time. With men, I wanted them hard as rock and ready to finish as soon as possible. I always found sex so exhausting. But with her, I could relax. I heard she had a bit of a reputation for turning straight girls. I had told **[REDACTED]** that one night when we were opening up about our previous experiences. He said it was one of the hottest things he'd ever heard. I neglected to tell him she had a buzz-cut and massive biceps. I didn't want to ruin his fantasy.

I bought wine for the celebration and lit some candles. I don't know why I bothered to make the effort every year, but I intuited this would be the last anniversary dinner we ever had, and it didn't seem right to break the tradition. I was impressed with his effort, though. He'd put on a nice shirt for a change and slicked his hair back. He looked handsome.

The awful thing about setting the table was that we had to sit opposite and look at each other. The television was usually a comfortable distraction, and this seemed far too intense. I placed the plates on the mats, the wine glasses on the coasters. I wanted to say Bon Appetit, but on one of our first dates I'd said it at an Italian and he laughed at me for being obnoxious even though I'd ordered a pepperoni pizza. Instead, I just said:

"Right, enjoy."

"Yeah. Right. Oh, fuck." He laughed nervously and looked up at me. I was amazed to find that his eyes were filled with tears. I stared at him, coldly. "I was going to wait till after dinner to do this, but I can't eat. I'm too nervous."

I lay down my knife and fork and leaned back against my chair, crossing my arms. I thought this was the moment of confession. The floods of tears. The begging for forgiveness. I awaited it so eagerly I could have screamed with joy. It was a privilege I never thought I'd be afforded. And if he was leaving of his own free will? Even better. I'd get to keep the house.

Instead, he reached into his pocket.

"Baby, these past six years have been really magical to me. These past few weeks especially, I've realised how amazing you are, and I think it's time we take the next step…"

"Whose earrings are these?" I blurted out. He looked baffled.

"I don't know, do I? I thought they were yours."

"Well, they're not."

"Oh," he said. "Okay."

It took a second to realise what was happening, and I moved fast so as not to lose my sense of indignation.

"You're not even on one knee," I scoffed. He moved his chair, went to kneel down, tentative in a way I'd never seen him before. "Oh for god's sake, get up," I said.

"I don't know what you want!"

"You're having an affair, aren't you?" I said.

"What? No!" We were silent for the longest time. I couldn't think of where I wanted this to go. I waited for the relief I should feel, but it didn't come. Eventually, he broke the silence. "When would I even find the time to have an affair?"

He was right. We never slept in separate beds. We never took separate holidays or went on business trips away. Every night for six years, more or less, the same bed, the same car driving to the same office, the same car back, the same sofa in the same living room, the same, the same, the same, until I thought I was going mad.

"Oh God." I hid my head in my hands. "I wish you'd been having an affair. It would have made this so much easier."

"Made what easier?"

"[REDACTED]," I said, in the calmest tone I could manage, "these past six years have been really stale for me. These past few weeks especially…"

"Oh, for fuck's sake," he said, throwing down the ring box. "You are all over the place. You want to settle down. You want me to be more romantic. And then when I try, this is what I get?" He grabbed his coat from the back of the chair. "I'm going to stay at Pete's for a while. When you decide what you want, let me know."

He slammed the door behind him. I wondered if I should be crying. I wondered also if I should be worried he was heading over to the new receptionist's .

Moving to the floor, I opened up the ring box. There it was. Classy and subtle, though perhaps a little plain. A single silver hoop tucked up in a bed of velvet. I felt my earrings and smiled. They were still there. Two hoops were better than one.

"I know what I want," I whispered to myself. Because I'd known from the beginning. "I want to be Cyndi Lauper," I said.

Oh, Rats

Marjory was on her knees when she found the dead rat under her bed. It was starting to bloat already, and although she hadn't smelt it before, she could smell it as she crouched down—that rich, earthy scent of decomposition. Its eyes were still open, staring at her as though conscious and feeling the pain of disintegration.

It must have been there for at least a week. Rats never came into the house of their own volition; Whiskers always dragged them in by their necks, and Whiskers had been dead for a week now, having been found flattened by the side of the road, the victim of a rogue tractor and a misguided sense of self-assurance. Marjory was slowly adjusting to life on her own, but it had been difficult, despite her stoic lack of tears.

She reached her arm under the bed to grab her pen, which had rolled uncomfortably close to the rat. She could've found another, but she was already late, far too late to begin dealing with corpses, and she had to get to work. She liked to be earlier than her boss, liked him to walk in and find her sitting behind her desk in un-laddered tights and a neat bun. "Good morning, sir," she'd say, trying to keep that balance between professionalism and mild flirtation which she knew most employers liked. Mr. Hopkins never answered her with anything more than a grunt. Marjory wasn't sure if she'd really get into trouble for lateness, but she liked to think that she would. Mr Hopkins' supposed temper and high standards were often related to Whiskers while Marjory rushed about in the morning. "Can't be late for His Majesty!" she'd say while the cat slowly blinked at her, lying in between the bundled-up covers.

Marjory got into her car and tried to put the decomposing rat out of her mind. Of course, it was all she could think about. She wished she'd swept it up there and then because now all day all she would think about would be the vermin she had to deal with when she got home. It would have been easier if it was a mouse or a bird, but there was something about the size of the rat, the sickening thickness of its tail which made her squeamish. She remembered hearing horror stories about rats taking babies from their cribs at night. For once, she was grateful not to have a little angel of her own.

She got to work early, as always, switched on the lights and computer and settled down behind her desk. She'd taken down the "Is It Friday Yet?"

poster tacked on the wall because Garfield's grumpy face reminded her too much of Whiskers, and she found herself with a lump in her throat every time she walked into reception. Now, she realised that the lack of the poster actually made her feel just as despondent. Mr. Hopkins hadn't noticed, which Marjory found upsetting. She was hoping that he might, and she could explain the loss of Whiskers, being wonderfully strong, maybe shedding a tear, but laughing all the while and calling herself silly. Then maybe he would take her out for dinner to commiserate, and they could bond over their irritating clients with their desperate halitosis. And maybe, just maybe, Mr. Hopkins could take hold of Marjory's hand and say something along the lines of: "I just don't know how I'd cope without you, Marjory," and she, again in that wonderfully modest, self-deprecating way, would laugh and say that surely she was just answering phones and it was nothing too difficult, and he would lean in close to tell her that she mattered so much to this company, and he wouldn't be able to keep going without her, and maybe then that's when he'd lean in for a kiss. She'd stop him, of course, talk about professionalism, but that tension would remain there and maybe at the end of the night, or maybe at the end of several nights, after a few more glasses of wine (which of course he would pay for— being the gentleman), they would both give into their desires.

But that didn't happen. Instead, he walked into the office looking bored, ignoring her at her desk.

"Good morning, sir," she said, smiling up at him, and again Mr. Hopkins grunted and closed the door behind him. And so, in an odd twist of irony, Marjory forgot about the rat and instead spent the whole day thinking about how it was a brand-new week and Mr. Hopkins *still* hadn't noticed the change in décor, and *still* seemed unconcerned with Marjory's evident devastation. She was annoyed he hadn't asked her why she'd eaten the whole tuna baguette at lunch, instead of wrapping up the last quarter and popping it in her handbag as she usually did for Whiskers (She knew that cats weren't supposed to eat mayonnaise, but what was life without a cheeky, little treat?). She drove home feeling drastically underappreciated, pretending to herself that it wasn't even *about* the poster, or the baguette, but the fact that she'd had to change a meeting for him after a cancellation, and he hadn't even thanked her. Marjory had reminded him it was time for his annual dentist check-up, and he'd simply waved her away: "I can sort out my own appointments, thank you Marjory." I mean, the cheek! He should be ever so grateful that she had some competence, unlike the secretaries that she saw at the doctor's office, gossiping about their weekends while they thought the patients in the waiting room couldn't hear, perhaps not even *caring* if the patients in the waiting room could hear. If those girls knew a lick of shorthand, Marjory would drop dead with shock.

She got home and dumped her handbag, avec bitten-down biro, on the kitchen counter, before pouring herself a large glass of wine. She wanted to order a takeaway but knew that she shouldn't after the full tuna baguette she'd had for lunch, so instead settled for a pre-made pack of spag-bol. She nestled onto the settee so she could watch her programme.

The problem, Marjory opined, was that she'd simply been born in the wrong era. Instead of going into work and eating out of black, rectangular Marks and Spencer's boxes, she should be galloping around the Yorkshire moors and gasping at the sight of young soldiers. Soon though, she missed the usual warmth on her lap and moved into a long and relaxing bubble bath, making sure to take the bottle of wine with her. By the end of the night, she was so tipsy and clean that she forgot all about the rat and collapsed into an unconscious slumber on her unmade bed.

She remembered at 4am, though. Woken up from her dreamless sleep with a pounding headache and a thirst she couldn't shake, Marjory recalled the rat that was rotting beneath her and felt sick to her stomach. She pushed a pillow over her head, willing herself to go back to sleep, but as is typical in times of desperation, the sleep just wouldn't come. She knew that if she got up, crept down to the kitchen, grabbed the dustpan and brush, walked back upstairs, and made an effort to sweep it up, then all she had to do was pop downstairs again and outside to the front bin in the cold and actually, upon consideration, it was a lot. But then it would be sorted, and she'd be able to sleep without all this anxiety.

But putting it in the outside bin would require getting her shoes on, and she didn't trust herself to hold the dustpan and rat steady from an out-stretched arm while navigating her shoes. Unless she risked going outside *without* shoes, but there was bird poo, and even though she lived in a nice, little hamlet in the middle of nowhere, there was no reason to think that needles couldn't be on her front doorstep, and if she contracted some awful form of hepatitis, she'd have to explain it all to Mr. Hopkins when they eventually decided they loved each other. The whole thing would be so mortifying!

Or else she could put on her shoes the first time she went downstairs to grab the dustpan, but that was problematic as she didn't want to mess up the carpets. Although, frankly, Whiskers' grey hair was so ground-in that her cream carpet looked constantly murky, something else she would have to sort out despite feeling terrible at the idea of erasing Whiskers' presence so soon after his death. Every time she willed herself to move, she felt convinced that moving was her Big Mistake and that actually, she'd been just about to fall asleep.

Eventually, Marjory did manage to stand. She remained in her nightgown staring like an insomniac at a spot on the carpet until her eyes adjusted to the dark, and she was convinced that she could see the rat's curled-up body. The slight curve, which may have been the rat, but was more likely just the shadow of a headboard, grew more and more distinct until Marjory could see teeth and claws in the dark carpet blur, and also something that surely wasn't, but looked like, a dead, open eye. She decided she'd do it. It would only take a second. She made it to her bedroom door near tears of frustration before she realised that this whole thing was silly. By the time she'd turned on all the lights, she'd be awake enough to go to work, even with the hangover, but she wouldn't be productive and the whole day would be a write-off. It could wait. She was getting herself upset because she was tired, and if she just stopped being so silly, she would have gone to sleep. Her mother always told her that her neurosis would be her undoing.

She crawled back under the covers feeling vulnerable, noticed the time was now 6am, and she'd have to be up and awake in an hour. She could taste the scent of rotting in her throat, but eventually, with eyes clenched tight, she must have slept because the sound of her morning alarm felt as shrill and upsetting as a hammer to the head. She snoozed it, over and over and over again.

It was practically time for her to be at her desk and she was still in bed. She rushed off, having absolutely no time whatsoever to deal with the rat, barely making it in before Mr. Hopkins with her hair seriously lacking the much-needed bobby-pins.

This became the routine for Marjory. Occasionally, she would have a full night of sleep because the previous day's exhaustion would catch up with her, and she would pass out as though knocked unconscious the second her head touched the pillow. The smell of the rat grew stronger to the point where she noticed it as she stepped through the door. It had started to seep into her clothes. She smelt it when typing at her desk, but she comforted herself by thinking she was simply going mad until one day she heard a client of Mr. Hopkins' ask if there was something in the walls.

The longer she left it, the more impossible it seemed. The rat had grown to nothing more than a pile of mush, but still at night in her exhausted, delusional state, she would see the teeth, the claws, the open eye. Marjory was tired. She was tired all the time. She began picking at her tuna baguettes, breaking them into multiple pieces which she'd place first in her handbag, then in her mouth, then in the bin as the smell of rotting from her cardigan would make her feel sick. She started sleeping on the sofa just to avoid the smell, collapsing in front of the telly. But even her period dramas were starting to lose their charm. She didn't have the energy to masturbate when half-way through the season the handsome side-burned man finally grasped onto his beloved and kissed her in the rain. Instead, Marjory stared at the television blankly, finding that she felt absolutely nothing but total and complete exhaustion.

She hadn't known it was coming, although it would have been obvious to anyone else. Mr. Hopkins took her aside.

"I'm sorry, Marjory, but you're just not pulling your weight," he said. "The clients aren't feeling as comfortable here as they should."

"How can I not be pulling my weight?" she asked. "Things have been getting done exactly as normal."

"Yes," he'd agreed. "But now they're done smeared with tuna."

"I can fix this," Marjory promised. "There's just one thing I need to do, and as soon as I'm done with it, everything will be back to normal."

And while Mr. Hopkins gave no indication of really believing her and expressed no interest in what it was that needed to be fixed, Marjory still felt emboldened by her decision. It was time for the rat to go.

She drove home, parked her car, and headed through the front door. Shoes still on, she grabbed the dustpan and brush. She walked up the hairy, carpeted steps, got down on her hands and knees, staring at what was now a ball of grey/brown mush. She poked it towards her with the end of broom, grimacing at the way the rat's fur was separating and coating the carpet. The vacuuming job would need to be intense. She went back downstairs, through the front door to the outside bin, opened the lid, and then stared.

The last bit was the easy bit, the bit which should have bought all the catharsis and the relief, should have untangled the anxiety she'd been feeling for weeks now. She stared at her wrist, willing it to flick, to drop the rat into the nearly empty bin. It wouldn't. She couldn't. Something about the greying fur just seemed too comfortable, too familiar. Under the open eye, beside the protruding teeth, she saw for the first time the rat's unrotten whiskers. Cautiously, she took it back upstairs, where it belonged. She placed it on the bedsheets, which hadn't been slept in for quite some time and stood back, happy with what she'd done. She would sleep in her bed tonight. She was looking forward to it. Marjory stared at the grey mush where the bulging eyes could still be seen. She willed it, desperately, to blink.

Respite

An essay in happiness gathered over the
course of five and a half summers.

1) "I think you're afraid to write a story with
a happy ending. That's what I think."[1]

2) One summer, when I was sixteen years old, I
had to get the morning-after pill. A few days
before, I'd been at a party where a boy may
or may not have had sex with me and may
or may not have used protection. I didn't
mention this to the pharmacist. He told me
that the fact I came to see him, showed that
I was sensible. I thanked him. He was very
nice about the whole thing. I don't think he
meant it, though. I thought I saw judgement
in the way he signed his name.

---

[1] As said by my sister, only partially in jest.

3) According to the NHS website, symptoms of seasonal affective disorder include feelings of "despair, guilt, and worthlessness."[2] In recent years, I've found that anything coming close to this description leads to an unrealistic self-diagnosis, which I then choose to wear like some horrendous badge of honour, allowing it to become justification for any bizarre or ridiculous behaviour I'm choosing to exhibit. It's a habit I don't imagine I'll stop any time soon.

4) One summer, when I was twenty-one years old, the doctors told me that I'd contracted a stomach ulcer. This led to an early termination of my work-contract and a depressing flight home. I spent the summer back in England, where I could binge-drink freely. That same summer, my friend had a nervous breakdown in Germany and was forced to return to her divorced parents' arguments and the expensive drinks cabinet she regularly stole from. We had a lot to bond over. In our small town, we spent our time at a variety of pub quizzes. A few old friends from sixth form still hung around, so we adopted them into our miserable, trivial pursuits. Mostly, we stayed in The Foresters

---

[2] NHS Choices. "Seasonal affective disorder." Health A-Z 01.09.2015, < https://www.nhs.uk/conditions/seasonal-affective-disorder-sad/> [Accessed 13.03.2018]

and drank aggressively inexpensive beer. "It's so nice in this pub that sometimes I feel like I'm going to cry," I once said. My broken-down friend responded in the kindest way she could.

5) "You need to chill the fuck out, mate."[3]

6) One summer, when I was eighteen years old, things were perfect. I had too much time and an exponential amount of reading. There was a huge lake near my apartment block, and I walked around it every day until I found my favourite blossom tree, a Japanese, watercolour dropped into reality. There was a beautiful cottage on the other side of the lake, and I swore to myself I would buy it whenever I had the necessary means. I'd settle down, breathe in the hot air, and read about death until I fell asleep against the bark. Sometimes, it helps to remember this.

7) After I took the morning after pill, I was scared to go home. Instead, I decided to meet another boy who had expressed some interest in me. He was significantly older, and I didn't know him well. He invited me over to his flat and I agreed. I wish I could say that I'd just been too stupid for

---

[3] As said by my broken-down friend.

self-preservation, but the reality is, I didn't care enough about myself to worry.

8) "I too wondered if the story was perhaps a shade too bleak. The arc has less suspense as we hurtle towards inevitable oblivion and the girl's fate seems inescapable. This risks a tone of schematic hopelessness."[4]

9) This boy was excited when he met me, and I didn't have to say much. It felt right whenever I did speak though, as though I was being thoughtful, insightful, or at least voicing something he had also thought before. I was used to speaking at boys, desperately hoping they would like me. Now, I found he was speaking to me just like that and it was easy to let him. Eventually, after we'd been walking some time, I asked him where his flat was. He told me we'd walked past it a while back, and instead we should just keep walking. It was spitting with warm rain, in the way of English, seaside summers, and I wondered what his angle was.

---

[4] As said by second marker. I sometimes wonder if she ever worries about me. Then I remember that there was someone who sent in work detailing the explicit rape and murder of an all-female pop-group, and I realise my self-contempt is frankly uninteresting and, more importantly for a creative writing course, unoriginal.

10) In cases of Seasonal Affective Disorder, doctors suggest a light-therapy box which can be used to simulate exposure to sunlight. [5] The flashing lights come in various colours, although they are often blue. While many people imagine that the sun's light is mostly white, it actually works on a spectrum of colours, meaning that blue lights may be slightly more effective for improving the winter blues. I refused to purchase one of these light-therapy boxes, and instead maniacally clicked a laser-pointer aimed directly into my stretched-open eye like some *Clockwork Orange* nightmare, believing I could mind-control my way into happiness. This did not work, and considering my persistent short-sightedness, I am now cynical about the possible benefits of laser-eye surgery.

11) One summer, when I was twenty years old, I lived in a hotel called Mrs. Panda's while waiting for my company to send me to work. There were palm trees that rained down the white walls outside, and a fleabag, ginger cat that always wanted to be stroked. Every morning, we met downstairs for cheap breakfasts and green tea. Everyone complained that this company had flown

---

[5] "Buying a SAD light," *SAD.org.uk.* http://www.sad.org.uk/buying-a-sad-light/ [Accessed 17.03.2018.]

us halfway across the world and couldn't even be arsed to find us jobs. It was nearly thirty degrees, and we could sit and read, or smoke, or talk to strangers and tentatively practice the words we didn't really know yet. If we all got bored, we'd go "exploring," which mostly just meant walking and looking at things because none of us had earned any money yet. "You've been here nearly a month now. You must be going crazy," someone had told me, and it wasn't a question, so I didn't correct them.

12) In our seaside town, the boy and I found a country lane. The rain had stopped and there was this chilly, conflicting feeling of sun on wet hair. He said we should walk down there, just to see what there was, and promised that if we didn't like it, we could always turn back. I didn't take much convincing. He talked a lot, and I didn't. I sometimes glanced at him, but mostly I just watched our tattered Converse on the gravel. After a while, I watched the sky. It was starting to get brighter now, and I wanted to catch sight of the rainbow first.

13) In The Forester's pub quiz, everyone knew each other's team names and we always came dead last. Our group would argue over answers ferociously, and then all turn out to be wrong. The lady who ran it was

called Vera. She spoke in a deep, Yorkshire accent, the type akin to childminders and dinner-ladies, which immediately made me feel in the hands of someone competent. Any money raised always went to something local. "Prostate cancer after our Dave, who's now in remission, thank you very much," and the people in the pub would all cheer that same "eyyyyyyyy" you usually only hear when it follows broken glass.

14) One summer, I forget the age I was now, but it was a summer and that is certain, an old friend of mine threw a family barbeque. For some reason, I was invited. I'd hung around the house that day helping with some art-project or other, and when the time came for tea, they let me stay. They were a hippie bunch who always had a lot of vegan food in the outdoor freezer. My friend's stepdad cooked his meat on a separate side of the grill and made disparaging comments about "not eating that veggie junk," then everyone else scoffed about the primitive mentality of men. My friend rolled joints while they cooked, and actually, I must have been around seventeen because I was old enough to smoke but young enough to be amazed that her parents did too. I had a couple of bean burgers and talked about how I loved the smell of summer. The smell of smoke and cut grass reminded me

of festivals, I'd said, and my friend's mum laughed and asked if I was sure I wasn't thinking about the weed. I didn't get high that night though. That night, there was a sense of control. When I did the washing up, I heard them saying nice things about me under their breath. For some reason, that mattered a lot to me. For some reason, it still does.[6]

15) It didn't take too long walking down that lane until we found a sort of tire swing, like something out of a saccharine American movie. Instead of a car tire, there was just a stick, not even long enough to sit on. "You're supposed to stand on it," he explained to me. "Your feet go here, and your hands go in the loop." So, I stood how he had told me to, and he pushed me on the swing. I found myself laughing, at first in an embarrassed way, before he pushed me harder and I laughed from the adrenaline. The loop started to tighten on my hands, and I got stuck. I asked him to stop pushing and he listened. When he loosened the rope, he asked if I was okay, and I said that I was fine, though the rope-burn on the back of my hand had caused the skin to break.

---

[6] As a result of my unusually pessimistic outlook, I cannot recall any positive feedback directly. I know what they said made me feel warm, that's all.

Something like that would normally ruin my day. For the first time, I wondered why I was so easily upset. We kept walking.

16) In reference to the sentence "therapy would not save her now." Comment, underlined. "Nor the writer of this story."[7]

17) I had to move city again. The summer was ending. We drank at The Forester's as we always did, and then to a terrible night-club shoe-horned into our quiet, market town: one storey, pub tables, strobe lights (although these lights, I noticed, could also be intended to simulate exposure to sun-light, and I spent my time staring at them so intensely, I assume I resembled someone who was perhaps not in need of any extra serotonin). Our group could only stand the place when we were already too drunk to speak. I told my broken-down friend that I had to leave soon. I was already going to be tired tomorrow for the journey. We were all so drunk, and I couldn't see straight, and staying here wasn't a good idea. She cried when I said I was leaving. "I don't want it to end," she told me. "I'm not ready to go back yet. I'm gonna miss the fucking pub quizzes."

---

[7] As said by a once loving partner who screamed obsceni-ties outside my house prior to his suicide. Easy to under-stand now why he was not an advocate for therapy.

I stayed out for another two hours, chain-smoking cigarettes and watching stars.

18) "It made me physically shudder."[8]

19) It turned hot so quickly that day, to the point that leather jackets were swung over arms and hoodies were tied around waists. I needed a drink, but we'd walked so far already, and soon we were under an unnecessary bridge, unnecessary because the stream that dribbled passed us was thin enough to jump over. He pulled a bottle of water from the bottom of his rucksack, handed it to me when I asked him to. The boy told me that he'd been adopted. He was in care all his life. The only family he'd ever known was a West-Indian couple, who ironed his clothes neatly and finally instilled some sense of discipline. They adopted him despite the care-system's warning that trans-racial families had a more difficult time with the integration process, and he should really consider other options. He told me that hearing the social worker say that was the first time he'd ever been ashamed to be white. In the hard-core, teenage society I lived in, all stretched ears, shaved heads, and Madeline McCann jokes, my political correctness was always taken for shrillness,

---

[8] As said by my friend, who now won't proof-read for me.

irritating piousness. I can't remember what it was I'd said, but it was something radically left-wing for a sixteen-year-old, possible redundant for anyone his age. It didn't seem to matter. He kissed me anyway.

20) In September, when I'd just turned twenty-two, I made new friends. It was a postgrad mixer for everyone who smiled too much and was scared of getting through the next year alone. They invited me to a pub quiz. It took a lot of effort not to laugh when they did, but I managed it. "And what..." the young man spoke into a squealing microphone, "is the capital of Australia? I'll say that again, what ... is the capital ... of Australia?" He had biceps that were too large for his t-shirt and his beard was perfectly trimmed. I'd met this speaker before as he led a tour round my new campus. He spoke in a perfect, RP, southern accent, and said things with the deliberate intention of seeming down to earth and "just like us guys." I hated him irrationally. He had nothing on Vera. It was still warm enough that I could wear a jacket instead of a coat and I sipped my beer and listened to my new friends argue.

"Sydney."

"It's not."

"Melbourne."

"No, it's something you wouldn't expect."

"It's Canberra," I had said.

"Yes," they'd said, "and wow, and how do you know so much trivia?" If there'd been a camera, I would've stared into it and winked. I would have had the canned laughter in the background, ready to go. Instead, I jumped into an anecdote about last summer and I didn't care that they all seemed to lose interest.

21) Sometimes, it's enough. It's enough just to know that the person who could have done that thing, pushed you into another spiral of self-hatred didn't do that, didn't even ask for it. It wouldn't have been hard to convince me. Or maybe it would have been. I'd stopped being myself that day, turned into someone I liked much more, someone who listened rather than spoke, and who only said what they really meant if they ever did speak. I was a person with confidence and could shrug off unimportant things. Maybe that day, I'd have put up more of a fight. It doesn't matter. I never had to find out. For me, it was enough to have a gorgeous day that stopped at a kiss. Sometimes, that's enough.

22) One February, when I was twenty-two, I woke up and the sun was shining. It was still zero degrees outside, but when I looked out of the window holding my mug of tea, it felt nice, like maybe something important was going to happen. I sat down and I wrote a thing called "Respite," flipping through memories like casefiles, searching for moments of bliss. It wasn't particularly well-written, but at the time, this was enough too.

23) "Isn't the quality of the writing something I should decide?"[9]

24) One thing they don't mention about seasonal affective disorder is that it's both temporary and horrendously permanent all at the same time. Amongst all the counselling and the lightboxes, you'd think they'd mention once that if you just trudge through the sleety, greying snow, and the freezing nights in black-mould houses, then eventually you'll get to a point in the year where you don't have to remind yourself that you don't want to die. Very soon there will be sunshine, blossom trees, barbeques, pub quizzes, and walks down country lanes with boys who only want to kiss you, and who you'll never have to see again. I don't

---

[9] As said by this reader, hopefully.

know if this would be beneficial for an NHS website. I don't know. I think it's beneficial for me.

25) "Why are you always so goddamn cynical?"[10]

---

[10] As said by everyone I've ever met to date.

The Old Castle

The Old Castle was falling apart these days. The bricks were loose, and the roof tiles were a death-trap. They kept the harsh, fluorescent lighting in the loos, and you could see the years of grime sticking where the sealant should've been around the sinks. Heavy makeup streaked the mirror until you almost couldn't see yourself, and the heaters in the smoking area never bloody worked; you either froze or burned your crown—there was no in between. They'd tried to spruce it up, but frankly, I preferred the place dilapidated. It held more of a charm that way when you were sipping your Bacardi and coke, or one of those new, awful cocktails they'd introduced with names like "Blowjob" and "Wet Pussy." "Gaping Arsehole" was a personal favourite. Not that I was drinking much these days. Tonight, I wasn't drinking at all, something I planned to announce quite proudly with the little cotton wool ball taped to my forearm underneath my usual toned-down, button-up shirt. You'd have thought at my age and with the prospect of sobriety, I might have preferred to stay home, but Friday nights are meant for dancing, and anyway, I'd promised.

"There she is," our Roxanne called over, her arms raised theatrically. Rox was already at the bar, a cigarette stuck to the dry skin on her lip. Ten years since the smoking ban and she still had to be reminded to take the damn things outside. It could've been dementia at her age although she still claimed to be a sensible forty-five (ha ha!).

When The Castle was more dismal, I found it much more beautiful. We made our own smoke-machine back then with the constant lighting up of fags. Course, everyone smoked in those days, and even if you didn't, it was important that you couldn't see what we were up to whenever lips would touch, a hand would find a head, the front of two trousers pressing together. Then if the lily law stepped in, you'd time to spring away before they caught you at it. *Is it a crime to dance now, officer?* Not that it'd stop them banging you up anyway.

"What's it going to be then, ey?" Rox asked in her usual husky tone. "They've a new one called 'The Sucker.' Apparently, it knocks you out flat."

"A water, if you please," I said with a hint of arrogance.

"What was that, ducky? I think you must've misspoke."

"Aha! But no, doctor's orders!"

"Pah!" Roxanne, forever the dramatist, mimed spitting on the floor. "Doctors. What do they know? I was told at twenty-five that my life-style would kill me, and now look." She waved a heavily braceletted and liver-spotted arm over her body, clad as it was in sequins and chicken feathers. "Fit as a fiddle."

"Aside from the hip-replacement."

"Shhhhh! Don't speak too loudly, darling. These children will begin to think I'm geriatric."

From her bra, she flourished a lighter and raised it to her cigarette.

"Oi, outside!" called out an insolent child behind the bar, flopping hair straightened flat against his forehead.

"I'm just testing it!" Roxanne answered firmly. "Come on." She picked up her cocktail and dragged me to the drizzly outside steps. I was grateful to step out, despite the cold. A gaggle of women (actual women, mind; not old queens like us) were dancing and singing on the newly furnished karaoke machine, butchering some of the classics. From the looks of their outfits and the willy-shaped straws, it was someone's bachelor-ette. I never understood why hen-dos gravitate towards The Castle so readily. Straight women always assumed that "gay" was synonymous with "fun," and while they weren't wrong in their assumptions, it didn't half ruin the atmosphere. But then, who was I to complain? These clubs weren't for me anymore.

"So, tell me, why the water?" Roxanne lit up a cigarette. I rolled up my sleeve.

"Because, my love, you are speaking to a blood-giver. A donator. A medical inspiration, if you will. My body might have saved a life today."

"Goodness. Who wants your blood?"

"As of this week, the United Kingdom, who have lifted the ban against gay men donating, thus allowing me to participate in much-needed philanthropy."

"Excellent news, my darling," Roxanne said sarcastically, sucking on her cigarette. "Although why you'd let those strangers perforate you, I will never understand."

"Oh please, don't pretend you're not a fan of perforation by strangers," I scoffed. "Well, at least you were at some point in your adolescence before the sinking of the Titanic."

"Droll," Roxanne replied, exhaling her smoke beautifully so that it curled in the tendrils like the stems of wilting flowers. She threw the tab end on the floor, ground it under her heels, which were noticeably shorter these days, although one daren't utter the words *varicose veins.* "How's my face?" she asked, splaying her fingers wide to frame it to the best of her ability. I remembered when Roxanne was the most beautiful man I'd ever seen, with high cheekbones and wide eyes the colour of coffee beans, and still beneath the powder, I could see that she was beautiful, more beautiful in fact, because despite it all she had refused to cower down and yet miraculously, against all odds, survived.

"You look awful," I said.

"Fantastic," she moaned. "To the powder room!"

The bathroom had once only been for men. Now, it was officially "unisex," but there was still the single urinal stuck stoically to the wall, the holes drilled between the cubicles, now mostly there for humour's sake, archaic decorations indicating long-passed debauchery.

"I can't see a thing in this mirror," Roxanne tutted, dragging her tan-coloured lipstick in the space between her liner. I leant between the sinks and watched her.

"You really needn't bother. We won't see anyone interesting tonight."

"Lord, when do we ever? But you never know. Anyway." She rubbed her lips together, separated them with a satisfying *pap*. "I choose to look ravishing for myself, don't you know."

The high-pitched hawks and squeaks that hurricaned towards the toilet door could only be the hen-do on a battle mission.

"Oooooh, I'm gonna wet meself," one dressed up as a ballerina (ambitious for her physique) cried out while barrelling into the cubical. The others waited outside, taking up as much space as possible and making it difficult to vacate.

"Mate, you look stunning," said an angel, a trifle condescendingly to Roxanne.

"Thank you, my love. You're not so bad yourself."

"Are they real?" asked another, pointing to her breasts.

"Of course!" Roxanne croaked. "I paid for them myself."

The angel leant forward to grope them from the bottom, cupping the padding as though comparing mangoes at a market. They all laughed raucously, and I wanted so badly to intervene and remind these women, with their bitten down cuticles and darkened roots, that our Rox was old enough to be their grandmother, and they wouldn't want someone fondling her in a dirty, old toilet now, would they?

"She's handsy!" Roxanne said, causing another cascade of cackles. "You should be buying me a drink first, I mean, really. I'll have this one then." She plucked the plastic cup out of a devil's hand and wandered off swigging. Through the plastic, I could see the mucky blue that meant it was all sugar and aniseed, a "Blowjob" if I wasn't mistaken. The women were in fits of hysterics. They'd be telling this story for years. It may make it into the Maid of Honour's speech. *I can't believe that drag queen stole your drink!*

"Vile," I said as soon as we were out of earshot.

"And think! Your blood can save one of them. Now that they've decided we're not all contagious to the touch. Now, let's shake them off that machine. Shall I go with Donna Summer or Diana Ross?"

"Don't tell me you disapprove," I said, rolling my eyes.

"Of Diana Ross? Why should I?"

"Of giving blood."

"Oh, I disapprove of anything that limits the consumption of alcohol, you know me."

I rolled my eyes, rushing to keep up with her as she stopped to flick through the songbook. Her long, ghostly strides were always something of an inconvenience for my short legs.

"But ultimately, this is an iconic day! Think about our *rights*," I said.

"What rights? The right to save their lives? Oh, I suppose it's all very noble, but wasn't it so much more *fun* when we were degenerates? We might have been hiding in the sewers, but we ruled them. This…" she stabbed her finger on the page, "is the one. Oh DJ…"

Roxanne scuttled off to make her request to the poor teenager who worked behind the decks, handing me her Blowjob on route. No doubt he had plans to be one of those musicians who played techno or electro or whatever they were calling it, and now he had to play some awful song from the fifties. I almost felt sorry for the chap.

When Roxanne walked on stage, I felt the lights went dimmer. It definitely seemed quieter, but then why wouldn't it be quiet? The place was near empty. The DJ began playing her song, but she waved him down.

"Not yet, darling. Wait for my cue." The music stopped. She smiled at the non-existent crowd. In that moment, I could see what she was picturing as she scanned her eyes around this vacant, plastic room full of shining lights and sticky drinks and overbearing heterosexuals. She was back, perhaps, to the way it was, when no one would have seen her for the smokescreen, and anyway, it was never good to see you but always *bona to vada your dolly old eek.* Back when everyone was your mother and the whole world, or at least the part we were in, was veiled in silk and lace with curtains drawn, and our blood was always spilt, but still, it was our own.

"Ladies, gentlemen, darlings," Roxanne began. "It's time for my final swan song." She gestured to the DJ. The trumpets began to play.

Hands Up

There'd been a heavy rainfall the night before which had kept Jack awake, but things were slightly calmer now. On opening the windows to the hot and humid air, he noticed that everything smelt fresh and earthy, but the clouds still hung heavy overhead and the wind was fierce. Jack had lived in Florida long enough to know that this meant the thunderstorm wasn't over.

He poured himself a cup of coffee from the pot his wife had made. Ordinarily, he'd drink it in his hammock by the water, but he settled on looking out the window, observing his land and feeling at a loss. What should he do now? His wife was at work. The kids were at school. For the first time in many moons, Jack had the place to himself, a privilege he was never normally afforded. It was such a shame it had to be under such ugly and worrying circumstances.

Jack retold himself the story. She'd been heavily intoxicated. She'd had a weapon. Worse than that, she'd been very slow in responding to Jack's demands. His training had prepared him for this situation, and he'd found himself in it a number of times. Jack never held back when it came to potential criminals. He'd rather ten crooks shot dead than one officer compromised. These days, there were a lot of people on the force who had all these dumb ideas about community building and rehabilitation, working alongside the vulnerable instead of against them. Jack went along with it and paid all the lip-service, they all did, but he wasn't so naïve as to actually believe it. He'd met a lot of toothless crackheads, knew these people were hysterical and unpredictable even at the best of times. There was no point working with them. They needed to learn how to behave before that would be able to happen.

He obviously hadn't known that she was fifteen.

Still, she had been heavily intoxicated and likely a drug-user, even if that hadn't shown up in the toxicology reports. She was holding something that could easily be used as a weapon, and worse still, she'd refused to cooperate with Jack's demands. It wasn't the first person that he'd had to shoot in the line of duty, although it was the first time he'd had to deal with so much fussing in response. He supposed that had to do with her age, and in a way, Jack couldn't blame the public for being so upset about it. His twins were nearly that age, and to him they were still little kids. But Jack had a job to do. You couldn't have drunken thugs dressed up like prostitutes parading the streets no matter *how* young they were. It's all very *cool* and *radical* to hate the police, but Jack knew that if people were left to their own devices, they'd be begging to have old-school coppers back.

His coffee had gone cold before he'd managed to take more than a few sips and Jack was irritated. His mind was preoccupied, but his body recognised that there was no use in falling apart. He felt like a hearty breakfast. If ever there was a time he needed home comforts, it was today. Jack decided he'd whip up some bacon and eggs.

The truth was, the public response had been hurtful. It's never nice to be called names. Jack knew who he was, and he wasn't a murderer. He wasn't a racist, either. Jack fiddled around with the stove and poured oil into a frying pan, flinching back when he lay down the bacon and it sizzled and spat back at him.

Anyway, she hadn't looked fifteen. Jack thought that she must've been at least nineteen. She had her hair corn-rowed down to her ass, in her extra-tight dress. She was tottering about in these silver little heels with straps around the ankles. What kind of parents let their fifteen-year-old daughter go out dressed like that? Jack wouldn't let his little girl be seen dead in that kind of get-up.

The official story was that they were all heading to a birthday dinner. Bullshit. No one dressed up like that for an evening at Chuckie Cheese with their friends. Thank God she'd had alcohol in her system. If they hadn't found that, Jack would've really been done for. Better still, her mother hadn't known, had sworn that her little girl had promised to behave herself. She seemed confused and disappointed by the report. The blood analysis poured doubt onto the girls' story, which would work in his favour. And one of the girls had a record for criminal damage. That helped, too. This whole thing could be seen as a cautionary tale about getting involved with the "wrong crowd." The bacon was burning. He tried to flip it round with the edge of his fingers, but it was too hot. He didn't know where the clamp-y things were (*what was it the wife called them again?*) so he settled on an awkward manoeuvre with a fork. The bacon was nearly done, and he hadn't even started the eggs.

She'd had some drinks. She was holding an unsuitable handbag that in the darkness had looked a little like a weapon, and she hadn't responded to Jack's demands.

The truth was that Jack had been getting bored. Since hitting forty, he hadn't been involved in any of the more rough-and-tumble work for a while, and there wasn't much going on. Everyone was inside these days. There were streets he could go to though, especially on a Friday or Saturday night, where you could pretty much always find someone to pick up. If it wasn't drunk and disorderly, it was prostitution, and most of the people walking home were only doing so because they'd just picked up. Jack knew that. Everyone knew that. They'd ride down the streets and people would glare at them, spitting on the floor as they passed.

Jack's partner was boring. A newbie. He said that if there wasn't anything for them to do, they may as well head back to the precinct.

"There's no point us being here. We might catch someone with a bit of weed, but that's not doing anyone any harm," he said.

Jack shook his head.

"Rule number one of being an officer," he began. "All crime harms someone. You need to keep your eyes peeled for what could be a potential problem. That's how you prevent the worst stuff from happening." Jack chuckled. "If these people knew exactly how much time we spent on *prevention*, they'd shudder at the thought of a world without us."

His partner (*what was his name? Abdel? Ahmad? The guys at the precinct just called him A-man, anyway*) gestured around vaguely.

"But there's nothing happening. Come on."

And almost as though summoned, that's when Jack sensed them as they stumbled down the street arm in arm, laughing raucously and clicking against the concrete. *Disturbing the peace.* That would do.

"Look here," he'd said. "And learn."

He stepped out the car and walked up to them.

"Evening, ladies," he began, "where exactly do you think you're off to tonight?"

The girls looked at him like he was a bad smell. His partner was still in the passenger seat watching him, slowly unbuckling his seatbelt with that disrespectful scowl on his face.

"We're just going…" one began

"We don't have to answer that," the Birthday Girl interrupted. She folded her arms over her chest. (In hindsight, she was slightly flat-chested, but then a lot of them were. It didn't always mean someone was a kid.)

"Ma'am, I'm a servant of the law so, like it or not, you have to answer me."

She rolled her eyes.

"Fine, we're fixing to get something to eat. Can we go now?"

"Well, hold on a moment, little missy," Jack said, smiling. "There's been reports of drug dealing in this area. None of you know anything about that, do you?"

"Nope," a different one said, this one tall and slightly aggressive. Later, Jack recognised her as the one who had the criminal record, although she looked hugely different in her mugshot, her hair puffing up in an afro instead of ironed flat.

"Well then, I suppose you won't mind if I search you?"

"You got a warrant to do that?" Birthday girl asked, and Jack started to get irritated.

"Right, that's it. Adam," he called over to his partner. "I'm gonna need some backup here. We have a couple of troublemakers resisting arrest."

"Resisting arrest?" he said, heading towards them. "What are we arresting them for?"

"Possible possession with intent to distribute."

"You can't do that," the tall girl said.

"Jesus, just let him search you," another one called out. "If we let you feel us up, can we go?"

"Fuck you, I'm not doing that," Birthday girl said. They started bickering amongst themselves and Jack got his hand on his holster, recognising the early signs of a hostile situation.

"Alright ladies, if you just calm down please and come with us."

"This is stupid. I'm gonna call a lawyer or something," Birthday girl said, and as she reached in her purse, she hitched it up her shoulder and oh hell, Jack didn't know. Maybe it looked like she was grabbing a weapon. As far as he could tell, she very well might've been grabbing a weapon. Or maybe she was just getting her phone. A phone so that she could film him. Put it online to get him in trouble for doing his job. Another idiot teenager trying to breach the peace, to spread distrust, to make it seem like he didn't know what he was doing. Jack just couldn't stand the thought of all this blatant disrespect. This was just the final straw and he supposed that's why he did it. He knew he could claim that he thought she was grabbing a weapon. He knew that Adam would back him up seeing as she wasn't being cooperative.

She was fifteen. She'd had a drink, but there were no drugs in her system. She had a handbag. She knew her rights. And Jack killed her.

It would've all been fine. At least, it could've all been fine if A-man hadn't been so difficult, refusing to lie about the bodycam and the details of the conversation. If there hadn't been CCTV footage that ended up leaked online. If she hadn't been fifteen, if she hadn't been, actually, from a nice family with good grades and no criminal record...

His bacon had burnt to a crisp. The three strands looked skinny and pathetic as they crackled. The eggs were whisked in a cereal bowl next to him, cold and sloppy, full of bits of shell, and Jack realised he had no idea how to go about scrambling eggs. He started crying. Jack rested his forearms on the kitchen counter and his head atop of them and sobbed and sobbed at his utter incompetence, wondering how he'd managed to mess up something that should've been as routine as breakfast.

The Tracks

It was too cold for stilettos. The ground was concrete and icy and there weren't any shelters or coffee shops nearby. The girls had walked to the only train station in their village and all they had was a sign and two platforms.

Lolly and Amber were alone. It was late, it was freezing, and very few people took advantage of this stop. The train was coming through soon, heading straight to the city, where there were clubs and drinks and people ready to kiss and touch each other. Lolly didn't understand why they had to dress up. It was fun when they were doing make-up and Amber was adding shadow to her eyes to make them look smoky, contouring cheekbones that didn't really exist yet, but now they were here, she felt silly. She didn't have any chest for a start and her dress kept slipping down. Amber looked fantastic, but she always did, with her fishnets and her lipstick and her high-heeled boots. She lit her last cigarette. Amber didn't look thirteen tonight.

"Why did we have to dress up?" Lolly asked.

"It's nice to look nice," Amber said.

"No one's going to think we look nice later."

"Yeah, well, we don't look nice for them. We look nice for us." Amber always had an answer for everything. It was her idea to come tonight, to sneak out of the house when no one was looking. "It'll be here soon," she said, her knee juddering up and down, anxious for the train to come. She didn't want anyone to stop her before it came.

"Do we have to go?" Lolly asked. She'd agreed to this, she knew. They'd planned for weeks, wrote down pros and cons lists, made up their excuses. They'd gotten ready together, laughing and dancing to their favourite songs. It wasn't often Lolly and Amber got to laugh in that house. Still, now the night was here, she was nervous.

Amber was sick of Lolly asking questions.

"I thought we were in this together."

"It's just with Dad…"

"Don't call him that."

Amber hated it when Lolly called him "Dad." Lolly didn't know why. She'd always called her foster parents Mum and Dad, whoever they happened to be. Sometimes it was what they wanted. Often though, it made them uncomfortable. There was always eye-contact, between the new mum and dad, or the mum and her social worker, or whoever it happened to be. It never included Lolly, this eye-contact. People spoke to her like they'd planned what to say in advance, tentatively, trying not to hurt her feelings.

"Sweetheart, maybe don't call us … that."

But Lolly never understood why. Everyone else had a mum and dad, why couldn't she?

The current Mum and Dad didn't mind what she called them. Dad didn't mind anything as long as the girls kept quiet. Lolly thought about how he would shush her softly if she asked a question or made too much noise. She'd asked Amber about it once and Amber slapped her round the face. Amber could very slap hard. Afterwards, she'd felt guilty. She hadn't meant to be harsh. Amber knew that Lolly must be hurting in the same way she used to hurt, so she decided to be nice. The girls stuck together after that. They did everything together. That's why they were here tonight.

Before Lolly moved into the house, Amber had tried to escape. She punched and screamed and bit arms until she left marks, but it made no difference. Her notes explained that she was a troubled child. She had behavioural issues. Amber was a compulsive liar.

But tonight, they were leaving. Soon, the train was going to come. Amber stamped out her cigarette, crushed it under her heel. She knew that she looked beautiful. She'd had fun getting ready with Lolly. The girls had had a good time. A nice day. Now the train was heading into the city.

"I'm not sure anymore," Lolly whispered, her eyes misting up as she saw the light in the distance.

"Come on," Amber told her. "Be grown up. Be brave."

The two girls stood together on the platform. They held hands. It was cold and they were shivering. In the dark, you could see their outlines, make out the profile of their hair, back-brushed to death, high-heels, straight bodies. The train was going through to the city, but it wasn't stopping at the girls' stop.

They stepped off the platform anyway.

The sun was turning the concrete a lighter grey, and Amber knew she would step off the platform soon. She would be with Lolly then. There were a few people around her now, old ladies mostly, heading to the beach. Amber wished Lolly was with her, asking some stupid question. She remembered Lolly's dark brown eyes and her wispy hair that always needed brushing. Amber missed her. She lit a cigarette with one hand; she'd gotten good at that now, and watched the train pull in. The old ladies got on, but no one got off. Then again, why would they? Amber stayed sitting on the uncomfortable, metal bench they'd hammered into the floor and smoked her cigarette. Soon, Amber knew with certainty, she would jump. She would be with Lolly and she would jump.

A hard tap, they called it, a smack, but never beating, never abuse. Those words came later from different mouths.

"She needs a good hiding," Lolly's mother said.

"Assault on a minor," the court had said. Lolly didn't understand why the words mattered so much when it amounted to the same thing anyway.

"Asking for a hiding" is apparently what Lolly did whenever she got in the way. Her life was scattered with these statements: "Asking for a hiding," and "this is what you get," and "I'll give you something real to cry about." So Lolly stopped talking. She didn't want to ask for anything anymore. The social worker called it "selective mutism." Lolly called it self-defence.

Sometimes, Lolly wished she was broken enough not to cry. She wanted to dye her hair black and prick herself full of piercings. She saw other kids in care that were damaged in a tough, artistic way, but Lolly was very slight for her age. Her hair was lank, and she had a tendency for cold sores. She cried a lot because she had to. No one listened to her when she used words so she resorted back to the thing she knew would work. When she stopped using words altogether, Lolly knew crying would always be there.

At age nine, asking to go to the toilet had proven too difficult. After weeping for close to an hour, she wet herself on the classroom floor.

"Special educational needs," they said at first. Then Lolly drew some pictures and they renamed it "trauma." In the homes, they told her that if she tried to talk, she'd have more chance of getting adopted. But Lolly didn't want to move from her first home. It was nice there. She had her tea made for her every day and no one shouted.

One night she knocked her tea into her lap. It was spaghetti. She remembered the orange stains spreading across her school skirt and staring at it blankly, not believing this had happened. She was desperate to go back in time just five seconds; that was all she'd need, and she'd remind herself not to be so stupid, and she wanted to cry but she was too scared, so she sat for twenty minute unable to move. The new mum—who asked Lolly to call her Auntie—saw the mess and laughed.

"Silly Billy, food goes in your mouth, not on your lap!"

And Lolly started crying so hard then that they had to take her clothes off for her and put her in the bath. The entire time she wouldn't calm down. Lolly wouldn't eat again when they tried to tempt her, and in the morning, she had a headache from the dehydration. But Lolly could whisper into ears after that. Soon, she could talk out loud. And then they moved her. And then again.

In every new home, new school, new street, Lolly would not speak. Some homes tried to bring her out of her shell; some were so packed with kids screaming and breaking windows that no one had the time. City to city to town to village to Amber. Amber in her black eyeshadow and tartan miniskirts. Amber who smoked cigarettes and knew how to give blowjobs and didn't ever need Lolly to speak because she had her own stories to tell. These were stories about sex with men in bands and future plans, and how to sneak vodka into school with Evian water bottles. Lolly didn't think Amber's stories were true, but she couldn't speak to say so, so she just nodded, and Amber grew to love Lolly.

Soon, Lolly was using full sentences. She was speaking about everything, but the one thing she couldn't speak about.

"An amazing improvement," the social worker said. "You really should be proud."

When Amber heard talk of adoption, she made the plan. She dragged Lolly into her room one day. She held her notebook, covered with song lyrics and doodled heats, close to her chest.

"You wanna hear another story?" she asked. Lolly nodded. "Okay, but you can't tell anyone. This is just for us."

"Okay."

"Do you promise?"

"I promise."

"Good. Because we always keep our promises."

"Amber, I'm not sure anymore."

They had landed on the tracks. Afterwards, Lolly began screaming, but the train was so loud that Amber couldn't hear anything except its roar. The tears separated Lolly's cheeks in two, white rivers in the orange foundation making the tracks look like scars.

The shape of her mouth said, "Amber."

Amber held her tightly, hugging her, waiting for the struggle to stop. Lolly snapped her stiletto wanting to get away, but Amber still held her.

"It's okay, it's okay," she'd said.

Then there was pain and the scream of the train above her, second after second of piercing wails that wouldn't stop, then a big, black nothing.

Was that what happened? Is that how it happened? It happened—that was all Amber knew. Somehow, this had happened.

A one in ten chance. There was a one in ten chance of jumping in front of a train and surviving and the chance of leaving without injury was zero which meant it hadn't happened yet. Amber would always limp, they told her, and she would never regain the use of her right arm. She learned to write left-handed.

Amber wasn't pretty now. Instead, she was brave. No one ever said Lolly had been brave. No one ever talked about Lolly anymore. That was Amber's fault. She never brought her up. Instead, she found it easier to talk about the arm. It was easier to talk about coping with loss when it was a loss she was actually coping with.

Lolly's mum hadn't been at the funeral, not her real mum anyway. A lot of Lolly's other mums had made an appearance, said the appropriate amount of "how awful"s and left. Amber hadn't made it to the funeral. She'd still been in the hospital where the people around her were trained in kindness, and they told her what they were doing before they touched her.

Now Amber was back at the train tracks and it was a nice day. She hadn't bothered to buy a parking ticket. She was waiting.

How had she lasted this long? What kind of life had she had? It didn't matter. This wasn't about Amber. This was always supposed to be about Lolly, who couldn't speak or walk well in heels and didn't live long enough to tell her own story. It was better to let people speculate, Amber thought, piece together their own stories from the evidence the girls would leave scattered on the train-tracks, in hospital records, in notebook scribblings that no one ever bothered to look for.

The sun was starting to set now, and Amber started shivering. She was happy to wait for the last train into the city, happy to finish her packet of cigarettes and watch the world go past until the dark set in.

"We're in this together, Lolly," Amber said aloud. Because they always kept their promises.

Snow Days

Isabelle was walking to the bus stop when she noticed the gravel glittering with frost beneath her. She placed her feet carefully, one in front of the other, keeping her eyes on those shiny, black, buckled boots, her white socks warm and snug over woollen tights. They'd be soaked through by the end of the day. Isabelle never managed to keep her feet dry.

Thankfully, her path was clear. The farmers had been down with their plows already to make sure they had access to the fields. Farmers started work at five in the morning and Isabelle thought this was awe-inspiring. She didn't know if she'd ever been awake at that time. It was a moment, to her, that didn't really seem to exist, a spooky place where the world was very quiet and very dark, where everyone wore gloves and spoke in whispers, watching their breath fog up the air as they breathed.

It was eight in the morning. The sky was bright grey, and the air tasted as cool and clean as toothpaste. Isabelle was always on time for the school bus. There wasn't any pavement when the end of her path met the main road, so the bus stop was jabbed into the grass, a pole with its tiny metal square that told people the bus-times (twice daily). Isabelle felt they'd installed it just for her.

She might have to wait a while. With all the snow, school may be closed, but she wouldn't know for certain until the bus didn't show up. Her mum would sit on the kitchen table in her dressing gown, nursing her coffee while listening to radio. She'd shake her head at Isabelle: "Nothing yet, love."

If the bus didn't come, she knew she could go back home and sit with her mum, watching cartoons on the TV, drinking hot chocolate. That would be nice, but secretly, Isabelle wanted it to come. She liked school. She liked the neat timetables and the designated hours. She liked hot lunches and the sound of bells letting her know when things were done. The library was the best part. It was warm and cosy and hardly anyone used it. She could hide in the corner on her favourite, comfy chair reading through all the books. Most of the time she didn't get to finish them. Sometimes, she'd pick up a book she didn't recognise and, with joy, realise that she'd already started it, and she could carry on from the middle. What mattered wasn't really the story. Isabelle just liked the *feeling*, the mystery of not knowing whether she'd be in a zoo this lunchtime or a circus, a broken home or an American farm, the past or the future, Africa or Asia or Antarctica. She held different tastes in the back of her throat when she read these books. She craved that element of surprise.

Isabelle liked her lessons. She liked her meticulously ordered pencil case with all of her colours sharpened to a neat point, her gel pens each smelling like different, sugary fruits. Isabelle wrote each day in a different colour. On Monday's lessons, she used blue pens. For Tuesday green. Wednesday was an orange day, then Thursday was black and Friday was pink. Friday and Wednesday were her favourite days. Thursday used to be yellow, but she could never read her own writing. Her planner was her pride and joy. She jotted down all her homework in tidy handwriting, and then she would cross through them with her red strawberry gel pen when she completed them later that night. Normally, she did it straight after school before tea, showing her mum what she'd learned. Her mum was supposed to be "helping" her, but Isabelle didn't need help. Still, they sat together and her mum would offer unnecessary advice like: "Don't forget to put the date at the top, love," and "Maybe those shapes would look nicer if you coloured them in," and Isabelle would nod seriously and immediately get to work, as though the comment was inspired.

The bus came. It was only a single decker because there were so few people from her side of the village who went to school. The students were raucous, and the floor was already slippery with muddy shoeprints. The chatter was loud and overlapping. Isabelle couldn't make out what anyone was saying. That didn't matter. They didn't speak to her.

Because of the snow, there was an aura of excitement. Everyone was wearing extra gloves and scarves, scraping snow from under the outside windows so they could pack it tightly into balls of ice. They weren't allowed to throw them in the bus, so they just packed them tighter and tighter until they could finally disembark onto the concrete playground, already sprinkled with salt. Then, explosion. Isabelle was glad she could skip out first to avoid it all.

A Year 8 boy threw a snowball at a Year 10 girl with eyebrows drawn on like upside-down Nike ticks, who immediately charged towards him as he scarpered. Isabelle watched all this from a low wall. It was cold and hard on her bum, even under her long jacket. She kicked her shoes against the brick as the snowballs flew around her. There was calm amongst all the screeching of girls and boys getting hit. When the bell went, Isabelle jumped down, enjoying the crunch of her feet in the snow. The back of her legs was numb. She walked along, leaving little horizontal stripes of shoe-soles behind her.

In her form-room, her teacher was trying to calm down the chatter.

"Right, coats off, please."

"Sir, it's *freeeeeeezing*."

"Get 'em off or you won't feel the benefit."

Isabelle removed her coat. She was right next to the radiator and, as always, placed her hands on the vertical bars until she couldn't stand the burning anymore. She'd use her hot hands to rub up and down her skin, turning her cheeks pink.

The teacher went through the register. They all practiced their variations of saying "yes," "here," "here, sir," etc. When he got to Isabelle, he just smiled.

"And Isabelle's here, good," and she smiled back at him as though in confirmation.

Isabelle hadn't spoken for a few years now. Not since she found the man. His body had been lying on the road outside her old house, and she'd screamed for help so long that she went hoarse. No one came. It was quiet in the countryside, after all. When she walked home from school at 3 o'clock, all the grownups were still at work. She'd never thought to check to see if he had a phone. On icy pavements it's easy to slide and crack your head open and that was something they'd all been taught at school which was why Isabelle made sure to walk so very, very carefully across the gravel. The man died, of course.

Because she didn't speak, she didn't have friends. Sometimes, loud and confident girls would try to take her under their wing, and she'd sit with them while she ate lunch, but afterwards, she always replaced her tray and sneak back to the library. People tried to bully her, but it wasn't much of a fair fight, so they stopped. Now, she floated along the corridors, always making it to lessons, always handing in her homework, but never fully present. The doctors said there wasn't anything *physically* wrong. Despite clear evidence of trauma, she didn't seem depressed. Isabelle felt she'd found a loophole in which she could experience the world without participation.

Outside the window a flurry of white opened from the sky. The snow came down and instantly stuck to the ground like Velcro, spinning in thick, fat flakes so perfectly and quickly that they seemed to blow horizontally. Isabelle felt a jolt of excitement in her stomach. While she was the first to notice, others soon crammed round the window and jabbered and pointed:

"Sir, look at that. Sir, we can't walk in this, Sir."

It didn't take long for the school to be closed. They realised that there was no way of continuing with lessons during a blizzard. The buses were called back, much to the drivers' discontent. Parents were called and asked if they could come and collect their offspring. Isabelle waited for her mum in the library, settling on the comfiest chair she could find. She picked up a book about schoolgirls and read for the first few pages, but then she stopped. She looked about her and took it all in, the smell of the books, the sound of the wind circling and hooting through the window space, the quickly darkening sky. She stayed like that for a few moments. It felt nice just to breathe.

Driving home, her mother comforted her, but there was really no need.

"I'm glad you're coming home," she said. "I worry about you on days like this. I know you don't tell me, but I understand it must be hard for you."

Isabelle listened to the crackly song playing on the radio—a gentle, slow acoustic guitar. She watched the white lines on the road disappearing beneath the bonnet of the car, and then rested her forehead on the cool glass to see the crooked, black trees softly struggling under the weight of snow like thick hunks of white icing. Her mother's hand was resting on the gearstick, and Isabelle placed her small pink-mittened hand on top. It was the only way to tell her that one day she would be fine.

To The Girl

I think I owe a thank you to the girl with long black hair—twisted and clipped up in seminars, trailing down her back in dresses and up my nose when she lay next to me at night. I miss the awkward kisses, fingers trailing down bodies' sides, each thinking, "Is this okay? Am I doing alright?" I miss kissing her thighs. Thank you to the girl whose gasps still play in my head when I am lonely. Just gals being pals.

Except, I also want to thank her because she *was* a pal, because she saw me cry and shake, with lumps in my throat, voice cracking and body in breakdown shivers. She saw my bitter hatefulness, my anger, and she stayed. She kissed me for the last time while it was still dark outside, both of us with morning breath (we'd had maybe two hours of sleep), and we said goodbye. That night she'd let me rest with my arm beneath her curving neck.

She called me on the anniversary of his death. She let me cry without reservation. She maybe didn't understand, but she tried. She knew there were feelings more important than jealousy. She listened. She empathised. She was reasonable. I think that this, more than anything, is love.

I thank the girl for showing me that intellect doesn't have to be cutting and cruel, that there can be talent without unjust superiority, that listening is valuable and kindness is free. I thank the girl for honesty, for building boundaries, for frank discussions about our feelings. I thank the girl for unceasing support, for love and loyalty, and for offering me beauty amongst so much pain. I thank the girl whose kisses remind me that I am a human, the girl whose body dips inwards for my arm's perfect placement, who speaks to me so gently that even in my worst state I know that we are safe.

Perhaps if the world was as kind and open-minded as she is, if there weren't so many oceans between us, we could still be together, forever wrapped up under bedsheets, tasting necklines, feeling pretty. Life doesn't work that way, but I can thank her.

So, to the girl:

Thank you. I love you. You're welcome back anytime.

Your Son's Good at Times Tables

I'm sorry. I really am. I know my general demeanour isn't threatening (sad eyes, nose in book, phone placed on tray-table—which I continuously and neurotically check), but still, I know I can't look very approachable. You're traveling with your son, but you don't look like a mum. There's no lines round your mouth, no tight-lipped expression, and he looks maybe around nine or ten, but you can't have reached thirty yet. I like your pink hair and your denim dungarees. I like your Doncaster accent. I like the way you speak to me through him.

"You never know, Ross. Maybe someone will talk to us. All the best stories start with strangers on trains."

I sink my chin down farther, head in book, head in book. I try to think of something worthwhile to say, a half-decent way to accept this invitation to speak, but by the time I think of something, the moment's passed. We're the only ones on this carriage, so you must be talking to me. I consider saying something ironic like:

"Do you want me to speak? Because if you want me to, I will, but I'm far too shy to initiate anything interesting," in a way that I hope will be vulnerable and yet charming, and then the onus will be on you to think of something interesting (which realistically, I feel like it should be anyway), but instead I say nothing. By the time I've plucked up the nerve, the well-rehearsed line would be awkward instead of endearing (and would it really ever have been endearing?). But deep down, I don't think that trains are for conversations. They're for scenery and listening to loud songs through headphones. They're for catching up on books. They're for introspection. I do wish that I could speak to you. If I were able to, I would. My chest has been feeling tight ever since you sat down and told your son that all good stories start with strangers on trains.

This carriage is hot because the air conditioning is broken. This is why we are the only ones here. Everyone else left for other carriages, but we three do not fear sweat or isolation. Perhaps we have a lot in common. I would know if I spoke to you. But then again, why sit in the emptiest carriage and attempt to evoke conversation with the only person there, a person looking deliberately unapproachable? Find a full carriage! Speak to full tables of diverse and weary travellers. Leave me be. And yet I know if you left now, I'd be heart-broken. I need your attention, but I hate recipro-cation. I'm shy, you see? You turn to your son.

"Do you know how to work out a percentage?" and he doesn't, so you tell him. You're showing off your intelligence. You ask him about fractions and he's slightly unsure. You demonstrate because it's much easier for you to explain numerators and denominators than it is for him. Ross com-pensates, though. He shows off too because he's very good at times tables. You throw the numbers at him like ninja stars, and he bats them away effortlessly. Correct, correct, correct. You say:

"Bloody hell! You already know all this. I'm learning that in college!" which lets me know you've gone back to studying, and I want to tell you (while understanding that it might sound condescending) that I think you're really cool, and that balancing ambition with personal responsibilities is hard—college is tough enough at seventeen when you're middle-class and child-less. Maths is solid at A Level. I took essay-based subjects, and judging by my inability to write a concise sentence, it's clear to see I didn't learn too much. My brother and sister dropped maths red-hot, and they were brighter than I am, so I stayed away. I think you're brave. In fact, I know you're brave because you look around for con-versations on an overheated train while I am gut-less. But thankfully, the moment has long passed, and you're helping your son with maths. He's really pretty bright, you know. I'd know. I teach.

Perhaps he'll be alright with tough A Levels maths, just like his mum. I'm relaxing now contentedly, pretending to read while listening to your revision session. I assume this is the end, and while I'm sad I did not speak, there's relief and calm surrounding me.

It's rare for anything of note to happen on a Northern Rail train, but things keep coming. The smell of burning rubber permeates, you catch my eye and say:

"Do you smell burning?" and I go:

"Yeah, like burning rubber," aware that I'm responding too quickly out of keenness, and you respond:

"Yeah."

This is my moment to accept human communication, to build on my relationships, to finally feel more connected to the world, and all I have to do is say something like:

"By the way, your son's good at times tables," but I get too nervous, and I think of something perhaps more acceptable, more mundane. Something like:

"Well, I hope the train doesn't break down," so it's connected to the smell. Or even something non-vocal: a smile, a shrug, an eyeroll, something demonstrating that I am a person capable of interaction. I turn back to my book. I am so painfully predictable. I check my phone again because I crave contact. There's nothing. Of course, there is nothing.

You turn to Ross.

"Looking forward to an adventure, mate! I hope someone talks to us."

I look at you, but you're looking out the window which makes the words stick in my throat, a clichéd expression, but isn't it true? Like I've swallowed them the wrong way and I'm scared I'll cough and choke. I put down the book to say something. I wait too long. I check my phone.

We're pulling into my stop soon. For some reason, I think your journey might be significantly longer than mine is. I think it'll be more tumultuous, and you might have farther to go. I want to remember your comforting accent, your pink hair, black dungarees, and bright eyes staring out a window. I see your son's short, blonde crew-cut, his clothes well put together, his face looking so grown-up.

I stand up too soon. I want to say things to you. I have a speech I'm in the process of memorising. It will go something like:

"I'm sorry. I really am. I'm sorry that I didn't speak to you. It's not your fault. I'm cripplingly insecure and have these terrible moments of shyness where communication seems like a physical impossibility, but you should know I think a lot about you from what little I know, and by the way, your son's good at times tables."

But I realise soon that this is far too much and reveals parts of me that I'd never dare to say to you, so instead I edit down and think:

"Your son's good at times tables." That's all I'd have to say. I'd never see you again, and if you found it strange, it wouldn't matter.

"Your son's good at times tables," and this kind of compliment is valuable and good for kids to know. I want him to feel proud of himself, to have some self-esteem because kids deserve it.

"Your son's good at times tables," a normal, healthy sentence that does no one any harm and at worst could indicate eavesdropping, and all I'd have to do is say:

"Your son's good at times tables…"

But I don't. I hover by your seat, adjusting my bag. I say nothing. I think the anguish shows on my face. I move on and disembark from the train, and this is painful. I have left you. I've failed tragically. You'll recover. You'll find someone interesting at the next stop, and you may even speak about me, feeling amused at what you'd perceive as unfriendliness and irritation, but I will agonise about how pathetic I am for weeks. I cannot get past my own self-consciousness for long enough to say, I think you're very brave and your son's good at times-tables. But if anyone ever reads this, I would like them to know I saw a woman. She had pink hair and black dungarees. She had a son. He was clever. She was brave. I wish them all the best on their journey.

You say talking to strangers on trains is how all good stories start. Can silence make for mediocre ones instead?

An Open Mind

The tarmac wiggled up and down incessantly like a strip of grey fabric intended to symbolise water in a low-budget theatre piece, and I knew I couldn't cope with this in my current emotional state. I stared hard, willing the road to behave. It managed to still for a little while, but out the corner of my eyes, I could still see a defiant waver at the edges.

There's a lot of good in understanding your limitations. My regular cohort (all early twenties and riddled with ennui) often wake up in hospitals with pumped stomachs and pounding migraines with no recollection of getting there or whether or not it was intentional. In response, I always feel a smug sense of pride in knowing that I would never end up in their position. When I've reached the end of my tether (and I always know when I have), I go home, drink some water, and lie down to get some rest.

There are, however, some down-sides to this approach. I became aware of them when concentrating on the road with my fingers on my temples, having sensibly left the house party before the acid fully hit.

I didn't dare to check the time in case the face on my wristwatch started melting like some Dali nightmare, and as soon as I'd formed the thought in my head, I knew for certain that it would. I attempted to walk, but the floor rose and fell to meet me at a different rhythm to my footsteps. While I was certain I was stumbling, there was no reaction from the pedestrians around me, not that I would dare to meet their eyes. Instead, I focused on my feet.

I raised both arms like a tightrope walker, intending to take it all one step at a time, and in the process accidentally hailed a taxi.

"Where to, pal?" he asked, his window already wound down, and I knew then that what I was seeing couldn't possibly be real because the top of his skull had been sawn off completely and half his brain poked out visibly from the festering wound. The driver seemed unphased. The only creature I've ever seen to live in such a way was a pigeon fighting over chip scraps beneath our city centre's memorial plinth. I felt so sorry for it that at the time I considered stamping on its neck and only didn't out of fear of ruining my shoes.

I slid into the back seat, comforted by the leather and the smell of sickly, pine air-freshener, both of which allowed me to understand that this part must at least be real, a comforting thought in a moment of intense hallucination.

"Where to?" he repeated.

"Home," I said, hoping that would be enough, and without any further question, he started to drive.

"You alright, Chief?" he asked somewhat sarcastically, as though unaware of his own physicality. From the backseat, I could see that he was skeletal in appearance, with sunken cheeks and bulging eyeballs which only served to emphasise the tumescence of his brain. The only indication I could find that he had any skin were the yellow pimples erecting through it, one pinprick away from bursting orgasmically, cathartically.

"Are *you* alright?" I asked cautiously, having never been in this situation before and being unsure of the etiquette.

"Never better, mate. Never better."

The stop and start motions of the car increased my nausea, and I found comfort in closing my eyes, resting my forehead against the cold window.

"You're off early," he said to me.

"I reached my limit," I murmured, keeping my eyes closed, enjoying the darkness behind my lids until I remembered that closing your eyes allows the mind to turn *inwards*, and that was the last thing I needed. I forced them open with a start.

"That's sensible," he said. "Lots of kids your age don't know their own heads." I attempted a smile. "So, what do you do?" he asked me. I could see his thumb and forefinger make their way to the spots, eking out the yellow pus with the gentlest of squeezes.

"Not very much," I said.

"Oh aye, man of leisure, ey?" he asked me. "Or a student?"

I thought back to perhaps an hour ago, the house party I was tentative to leave with rolled up notes and lines that felt sprinkled with glass and sherbet, wine shot back like water (the only thing I could remember drinking in the last 24 hours) and the way that all of us collapsed onto beds in parties that never issued invitations, and I wanted to talk about my degree in fine art and the extent to which I believed creativity could alter the consciousness of the world, but in that moment, it felt disingenuous.

"Leisure," I managed.

The taxi driver nodded sympathetically as though he understood exactly what I was going through, which was funny because I could barely understand myself.

"It's hard these days for us lot," he said, and I nodded. At that moment, it really did seem hard for people like me. "Can't get a decent job. Course you know who they all go to?"

I made an assenting sound, attempting to say as little as possible. We went past the old cinema, white letters still manually handled above the door to emphasise its authenticity, the supermarkets that specialised in Polish food and illegal cigarettes, our local Chinese takeaways famed for gastroenteritis…

"All these bloody immigrants," he added. "I'm lucky you even hailed instead of getting in an Uber with bloody Masood or whatever." It suddenly occurred to me that I had both a digital clock and an Uber app on my phone, and in jumping in this cab with no money, I had undoubtedly made an error in judgement. "No good jobs for decent, British folk these days."

I couldn't bring myself to speak so instead focused on the therapeutic motion of him picking at his blackheads, oozing out white snakes, reminding me of the playdough I had kneaded as a child. I heard before I saw the slop of grey trickling out of his ears, plopping down and staining the shoulders of his (thankfully waterproof) Adidas jacket.

"Course, you can't say that these days, can you?"

"Your brain is melting," I tried to tell him, but he didn't seem to hear.

"Of course, it is," she said. I turned. Next to me there was a girl. Although it wasn't her, she reminded me so very much of *that girl* in my seminar. That girl who always talked a lot and never let anyone else get a word in edgeways. That girl who always thought there was an objective answer when we were discussing art, who dismissed me the second I opened my mouth because I wasn't underprivileged enough to have an opinion, apparently. That girl who got her eyebrows threaded but wouldn't wax her fuzzy armpits. She emulated Frida Kahlo, always drawing herself head-on with wonderful collages of flowers surrounding her. At one point, I thought that I might love her until I realised how insufferable she was.

I reached out to touch her, to stroke her hair and see if she was real.

"Oi! You don't just grab a black woman's hair," she said. "What's wrong with you?"

"Are you real?" I asked her.

"You have something on your cheek. May I?" she responded. She wiped it away with her index finger and then showed it to me. "Would you look at that? Grey matter. It's starting to get you too."

I felt my face in worry, but aside from my incessant sweating, there was nothing untoward.

"Why are you here?" I asked her.

"Someone needs to offer a sense of balance," she said.

"So, what are you going to teach me?"

"I shouldn't have to teach you anything. You can educate yourself, can't you?"

I heard another splat, but it was only a pimple hitting the rear-view mirror at exceptional pace.

"See, that's the problem with women these days," the driver said. "They've got this superior attitude. And you know what's done that to them?"

"Immigrants?" I said, with perhaps misguided confidence.

"Feminism," he responded in kind.

"Jesus Christ." The girl rolled her eyes.

"I agree," I said, glaring at her. "I prefer the term egalitarian."

"Yeah? What's that, then?" the driver asked me.

"It's *actual* equality and not just man-hating," I said, and I was glad I got to say it in front of the girl in a space where she couldn't just step away from my logic, although I was almost certain that she wasn't really there. She stared out the window. We passed the old cinema where they still put up the film titles in vintage block lettering, the cinema that was just opposite the flat I had escaped from.

"Are we going round in circles?" I asked the driver.

"Course, they don't wanna hear it when you say they've got it easy. Flutter their eyelashes and get away with anything."

"And yet fluttering our eyelashes will justify our rapes," the girl added, leaning forward.

"This is where you picked me up," I said. "This bit of pavement. We *are* going round in circles."

"Well obviously," the girl said. "That'll happen if you just keep turning right."

I felt as though we were, within this car, the needle on a record player, moving up and down while the rest of the world circled around us, receding and getting smaller and smaller and closer to completion. I felt the oceanic motion of the road, and when I looked up to see the stars, I only saw the horrid, orange blast of light pollution.

"This is awful," I said, feeling the vomit rise up my throat, quickly cranking down the window, an awkward, rolling lever motion, and I wondered how old this car was to not have automatic buttons.

"You should hear him when you're sober," said the girl. "Be grateful for the come-up."

The apartment blocks were spinning past me in smudges of grey, and the air was too cold on my clammy skin.

"You're going far too fast," I said. The driver didn't listen, and I felt the flecks of brain hitting the windscreen behind me as the wind caused the liquid to skim backwards.

"But it's like they say in the papers: there's a war on being white these days. Being *normal* int allowed now."

"Please slow down," I said, to no avail.

"Now, that's what I've been saying," said the girl, with something like a smirk.

"Why aren't you helping?" I admonished her. "Can't you see that we're on the same side? Can't you just be grateful that I'm at least trying to stop him?"

She smiled, this time a little sympathetically.

"Baby, when has thanking you ever helped us?" she said.

The car crashed violently into something concrete, and I had the horrifying realisation that it may have been the very floor that I had tried to still. I felt something roll, and my body seemed to float in space for minutes before a jolt let me know that we had landed. The brain of the driver was still dripping down onto the gearstick while his neck was snapped at an inhuman angle.

"That's the problem with 'em these days," he was managing to mutter. Though it was hard to move, I turned my neck to see the girl. Her legs were crushed beneath the seat in front of her.

"I have to go," she said to me. "If they catch me, I want you to let them know I didn't struggle, and it wasn't suicide."

"What?" I asked, before I heard the sirens in the distance. "Thank God, we're saved!" I said.

The girl opened her door and collapsed onto the concrete beneath her. Slowly, she crawled away on broken legs, knowing it was safer to attempt to save herself.

The Family

Witness Statement #248

He never wore shoes during sermons. Brown toes curled up in the grass, his long hair brushed against his shoulders while he played guitar. His dark glasses meant he could stare at the sun without flinching. He was handsome. So human it was inhuman. Above human, you could say. Sometimes he'd stroke my hair while I was praying.

"Can you feel God?" he'd whisper. "He's in these trees, he's in this dirt, and he flows through me." Then he'd sing in a language that we all understood even though it wasn't quite words, and we'd realise that yes, it was true. He is everywhere. He flows through Father, and He loves us all. Then we'd sing too, all together, black, white, rich, poor—it didn't matter. The only thing that mattered was love. Father was love. His white vestments billowed around him when he danced *in front of us, and on our knees, we'd raise our hands and thank him for showing us what it meant to be free.*

We were safe with Father.

At first, there were only a few of us — the enlightened ones. We realised that they'd been feeding us lies all along. Corporate greed was out to kill our souls so they couldn't reach God in heaven. We didn't need material possessions. Father gave us everything. But they were always in the background, waiting. They were always coming. Father knew this. He'd dealt with them all his life.

"They want to lock you up for being free," he said. It was the only time I ever saw him close to anger. The group stayed silent for these speeches. "I was locked up all my life. As a child, they locked me up because my mother ran away. When they didn't find me a home, they put me on the streets, and when I learned how to get by, they slammed me up in prison. You just can't lock up a soul like mine. A soul like mine has too much to give."

Of course, we understood. Poor Father. I made sure that night I protected him. I held him, wrapped my arms around his waist. I felt the buzz of being purified again, an exhaustion that lingered and settled heavy on my eyelids.

It wasn't long after my child was born. My sweet baby girl with squinting eyes and a smile like Father's. I just wanted her to be safe. I would've done anything to keep her safe. The Family always protected each other. Together, we were whole.

Preface

My interest in the "The Family" began long before the amputations came to light. This is not unique. For a long time, the name was on everybody's lips. Satirical TV shows mocked them, teary-eyed civilians appeared on news segments claiming their relatives were being brainwashed, and everyone was desperate for an interview with this so called "Father" figure, despite any background information being suspiciously difficult to obtain. When the cult moved, the supporters who stayed behind found their faith dwindling, and eventually the entire group was forgotten. For five years, "The Family" was practically unheard of.

I continued my investigation sporadically, but all attempts to contact the sect proved futile. Requests I made for interviews were denied on the basis that: "Innocent civilians should not be subjected to investigation on the basis of hearsay." Their defensiveness seemed unnecessary, but thankfully, my persistence prevailed. I was one of the first to get the call when the initial statement from the Camp Leader was released.

Everything you read here is straight from the mouths of the survivors and the perpetrators of this trauma collected via statements, police recordings, and self-conducted interviews. I have made the personal decision to omit names to ensure that I can discuss the case as objectively as possible without sentimentality towards the victims.

There is one exception to this rule. According to police records Witness #99, a young girl moved to the compound only weeks before its shutdown, made a brief statement:

"Father loves us. I will not testify against him. What he did was for the good of The Family."

Identical statements appeared in the hundreds and due to the sheer number of victims, no one could press for more information for fear of wasting police time. It was years later when Witness #99 posted them a new statement, almost the length of this book, detailing everything that happened to her in the camps. While the police could no longer use it as an official statement, they allowed me to examine it. This statement has provided me with all the information I needed.

I dedicate this book to Witness #99 and thank her for her honesty.

Witness #99

This is how it happened, honestly and truly. Now that I don't have to lie anymore, I can tell you.

I can't tell you what they did with the arms because I still don't know. I'm often asked "why," and frankly, I can't answer. You never saw what they did with them. You just felt a faint aura where they were meant to be, like a line in your vision from glancing at the sun too long, or a shadow that disappears the second you looked at it directly.

It must have been late by the time they got back, but I remember it like it was morning. The grass was still crisp, and every time you breathed, your lungs filled up with mist. They were taking them mountain-climbing, to get them higher and closer to God. The kids who were scared of heights were allowed to stay in camp, reading and resting for other activities. The camp was for all the kids, the compound for the adults. That was how it worked, you see. I was writing in my diary when they came back. I wasn't really supposed to, but whenever people asked, I said I was writing messages to God. I wish I still had that diary. My memories aren't always reliable.

When I was told that we had to leave for the jungle, I was watching cartoons. You could do that on Saturday mornings because we didn't have church. I'm not sure if the tear-tracks on my mother's cheeks were real or if I imagined them later because I feel like they should've been there.

"Father's taking us away for a while. All the other children from church are going."

I can't have really understood what she meant.

"No thanks," I'd said.

My mother had never slapped me before that. She slapped me so hard my glasses fell off my face and light swam in my eyes. Being a victim is never as beautifully tragic as you think it'll be. You picture a hand lightly touching the bruise, your eyes wide and welling up with tears picturesquely. Actually, it's more snot and wailing because self-pity is never attractive. I try to remember that now, despite everything.

I still wasn't speaking to her when she dropped me off at the camp, even after the arduous journey. I would miss her, though. I'd miss her long skirts and her homemade jewellery. I'd miss the chaos in her eyes.

Camp Leader told us that something had happened on the mountain top. He asked us to be sensitive. His blonde hair was short then, and he looked almost young enough to be in the camp with us. Lots of girls fancied him, even though it was a sin. Maybe some of the boys did, too.

Johnny's amputation was the worst. I liked Johnny; he was closest thing I had to a friend in the camp. We were the only ones who laughed when Father spoke in tongues and mimed when we were meant to sing. He was older than me and his fringe always dangled in his eyes because it grew too quickly. Most children were cut at the elbow, but his cut was right at the shoulder. It didn't look like a clean amputation. It looked like a deformity, a withered flap of skin with no bone. He caught me looking once. He was flipping through a book, but he couldn't really do it right. He struggled to keep it open and when he'd finally got comfortable, he'd have to turn the page and place it back down on the floor.

"I'm sorry about your arm," I said. It was a risk to say that. He sort of shrugged.

"Nothing I can do about it now."

I thought it was a nightmare at first. I couldn't control my actions. I did whatever they told me to, even when I found out that we were staying in the camp forever. But there was another me, a real me, vaguely aware that I was dreaming, knowing that everything that was happening here wasn't quite right.

I thought "they" had done it. I think that's what everyone else thought too, but it's difficult to say since no one ever spoke about it. One girl asked the Camp Leader in a whispered confession what had happened. Camp Leader smiled and told her to have trust in The Family. Later, they cut her, too. We realised then that it wasn't a one-time thing. No one was safe.

Our parents made food for us in the compound, and Father made sure we had all the supplies we needed, but Camp Leader sometimes let us go into town as a treat. We never had any money, but we could look around at the shops, and it gave us time to talk away from all the adults. Sometimes, I'd steal a few pens for my diaries. I knew stealing was a sin, but I thought God would forgive me. It was a four-hour journey into town, so we weren't allowed very often. I was one of the lucky ones. I could go nearly every time a trip was planned. The amputees were never allowed, even the older ones. There were some in the camp that were still babies and Camp Leader had to look after them all. The whole time I was there, I saw more and more flood in, stumps slapping by their sides, scrambling through the jungle earth with brown feet.

I remembered TV adverts from the old days about people in Africa with no food or water. They always played sad, piano music and focused the camera too long on the children's eyes. It wasn't exotic in the camp. When it was happening in front of you, it was just irritating. Maybe I didn't look in their eyes long enough to feel sad. And I hadn't heard piano for years.

Witness Statement #1: Camp Leader

Police Officer: This interview is being tape recorded. Please will you state your name for the machine?

Witness #1: I'd rather not.

Author's note: These extracts were recorded in 1992. The Camp Leader, who we will refer to as Witness #1, had just come forward.

#1: It was a woman's arm, covered in tattoos. No one had tattoos in the camp, you understand. And children can't get them. It made no sense.

PO: Tell me about the amputations.

#1: We weren't supposed to cut adults.

PO: But you amputated the children?

#1: I'm here about Mary.

PO: Humour me for a moment. Why did you cut off children's arms?

#1: Family must prove their loyalty to the cause and compensate for their sins.

PO: What sin?

#1: Every child is born in sin. The Lord does not condone fornication.

PO: This is in the Bible?

#1: Father told us.

PO: Of course.

#1: The children have the choice to be cut. They may not know they have the choice, but they always choose it. Getting cut stops the pain. When they're in heaven, they'll thank Father for what he did to them. For them.

PO: And you believe that?

#1: Father said children are vulnerable to lies and corruption fed to them from a TV or computer screen. They'll see the world outside and try to leave. If anyone found out where we were, they'd never let us be. We couldn't let the children run off and tell others. They need to understand the world is cruel. Evil is everywhere, except The Family. The Family just want them to be saved. Salvation requires sacrifice.

PO: But you're telling us where The Family are right now.

[A long pause.]

#1: This is different. They started cutting adults. He killed... That's against the rules.

PO: Did Father teach you the rules?

#1: I was his understudy. He taught me things no one else knew.

PO: And when you were cutting the arms, did he tell you what to say then, too?

#1: Yes. I told them their arms were gone for the greater good. It was something they needed, and in the end it would be better, but we couldn't tell them why. The longer they kept a secret, we said, the sooner they would be able to go back to their families and the longer they could keep the other arm. "And you don't want to lose both arms, do you?" [A slight laugh followed by a cough. The sound of the police officer's scribble is continuous.] You had to keep smiling and convincing them it was all okay even when they were passing out in chairs, and you knew they'd probably die from the blood-loss. [The scribbling sound stops instantly.] But that didn't happen often.

PO: There were deaths?

#1: It was collateral damage.

PO: Infanticide.

#1: But never with the adults.

[Pause.]

PO: Which arms did you take? Right or left?

#1: Cutters never checked. If it was the less dominant one, we said, "we did this because we loved you and we wanted you to succeed." If it was the more dominant one, we had a line too: "We knew you were strong enough to cope with this. Not everyone is. You're one of the special ones." They didn't cry often. The tears came during the cutting, but after that, the shock was too much. They accepted it after a while though. Getting them to accept it was easy.

PO: The children accepted this?

#1: Not all of them. Johnny was the first to challenge me. He was slightly older, had this long hair that made him look like a teenager. He probably should've been in the compound instead of the camp or being taught by Father like I was. Johnny was unlucky, though. He kept screaming, "How could you do this? You won't get away with it!" all that kind of stuff. It was our fault. The drugs hadn't been as effective as they should've been, and it was clear he was in pain. His eyes kept flinching away from the light and he squirmed constantly. Blood seeped through the bandage. It was horrible. [Pause.] See, I thought that was where the tattoos came from, someone slipping up and slicing an adult. If it happened to Johnny, it could happen again.

PO: How did Johnny get cut if he was too old to be in the camps?

#1: His mother had lied. She'd wanted to prove she was willing to sacrifice even though she didn't have to.

PO: Do you remember what you said to him? To Johnny?

#1: It was years ago, but it's always the same. Something like, "You need to be strong here. This is for your own good," you know. But he screamed anyway. I never saw so much hate in a child before. I called the cutters, and they took him back and sliced him up to the shoulders. I told them, this time, to anaesthetise properly. That was only the first trial though, and aside from that hiccough, it was incredibly successful. The children were more receptive than we thought they would be. Father was proud. That's why he gave me permission to enter the icebox where the arms are kept. Whenever I wanted—that's what he said. That's how I saw the tattoos. I was one of his favourites.

PO: He told you that you were his favourite?

#1: He thought of me as his brother, his son, his apostle. He loved me and trusted me the most.

[His voice breaks towards the end.]

PO: You're doing the right thing here.

#1: I need to stop answering questions now. Really, I need to stop.

Witness #99

After about a year, we stopped being allowed into town on our own. Camp Leader would accompany us everywhere. This was because I'd gotten lost once. I hadn't meant to. I'd just gone the wrong way, confused my lefts and rights. I got scared, the panicky sort of scared where you're struggling to breathe, and you can't cry because the lump in your throat blocks the air. I saw people in a shop who I thought must've been Family, but when I got closer, I knew I was wrong. The woman had stars down her face over a big, red patch of swelling. I felt anxious when I imagined those stars on her face, forever. A machine hummed in the background. The man was drilling her arm. She was practically covered in tattoos by that point, but he didn't have any. The light made his skin look yellow.

"Aren't you a bit young to be here?" he asked. It wasn't really a question.

"I'm not supposed to be."

"Are you lost?" He didn't look up from the arm when he spoke. "Do you know where your parents are?"

"No," I answered. "I'm in the camp."

"Ah..." the girl with the stars on her face moaned, and I couldn't tell whether it was in pain, recognition, or pleasure. "You're part of The Family. Welcome, sister."

"You're at the camp?" I asked. I knew she wasn't; she was clearly too old. But she was thin like all of us, slight and small, a bird of a human.

"I'm in the compound. You'll be there one day."

"Thanks to the kindness of Father."

She didn't nod. The drilling kept on and made me feel strange, like I was dreaming and the sounds in the real world were trying to wake me up. My head span. To this day, I don't know how I stayed so much in control. For a long time, I pretended I'd forgotten what she said to me.

"I know what they do to you in the camps. I know about the arms." I kept my hands steady, smiled even.

"Father forbids us to talk about those incidents. Had you forgotten?"

She sat straight up; the needle flinched.

"Jesus," the man cried out, wiping her arm with tissue. "You've made yourself bleed."

The lady grinned at me with teeth that now I picture caked in blood. They won't have been. That's just the image I have. Wide eyes with dark bags. Matted, dirty-blonde hair and wonky, ink stars scarring her red cheeks. The blood creeping through the gaps in her teeth were like my mother's tear-tracks. Maybe, I pictured it because I thought she was dying. Maybe because I thought she was dangerous.

"You have to run away," she said, "that's what I did. He told me my body was pure and sacred. He told me it belonged to him, for he was part of God. I'm taking my body back and I'm gonna get my baby. Then I'm going to tell the world, everyone's gonna know. Nobody's taking my baby from me. Nobody's mutilating my baby."

The man with the needle kept drilling.

"I need to find my way back to the camp now," I said quietly.

She stared at me for a while, her face flickering with hurt. I couldn't let her know I believed her, but I did. The only reason I'm still alive was because of that hope burning away in my gut.

"I'm coming back for you," she told me.

I don't know why but I nodded.

"Okay."

Eventually, Camp Leader found me wandering the streets. He didn't punish me much, a slap on the wrist. I hoped the lady with the stars on her face would come back for me, but when the days went into weeks went into months, I stopped remembering what it was I was waiting for. Then I made myself forget her. It was safer to forget.

Witness #1

#1: I don't justify my crimes. Really, I don't. I know amputating all those children was wrong.

PO: So why did you do it?

#1: I asked Father not to make me. Asked if I could move onto the compound after Johnny's cut. I told him that I understood we had to ensure complete obedience, but he just shook his finger at me and said, it's not obedience. It's retribution. For the good of The Family.

PO: Father wouldn't let you join the compound?

#1: He wanted me close to him. Being a favourite, it was good and bad. I knew he'd never hurt me. The entire time I was there he never beat me or tested my loyalty. My parents moved to the jungle when I was sixteen, and I'd been with him almost my whole life. They wanted to sacrifice me to the camps, but he saw right though them. "Lying is a sin," he'd said. They got on the floor, grovelling and apologizing. I was too old for the camps, too young for the compound. He put me in charge of the children, made me his understudy. I was lucky. Father was good to me.

PO: You said being a favourite was good and bad?

#1: Some parts weren't so great.

PO: For example?

#1: Well, he was doing it to save me. I know that. He didn't want me to suffer from the lack of it.

PO: What did he do to you?

#1: Some men were castrated. By choice of course. I asked if I could be, but Father wouldn't permit it. "God wants you whole," he'd said.

PO: Did he touch you sexually?

#1: There were girls who got pregnant, and he'd forgive them. Rub holy water on their stomach and remind them all that God speaks through him and he has the power to forgive. But then the babies had to go to the camps. To compensate for the sins, you know. I guess they were his sins too. I try not to think about it.

PO: What makes you think they were his sins?

#1: He liked big eyes and blonde hair.

PO: What did he do to you? What's making you so sad?

#1: Nothing. Nothing bad. I mean, yeah, I feel sad about it now obviously. Sad about the other girls, if anything. I thought I was supposed to be special.

Author's Note:

No one ever called it what it was directly. Purification, they said. It was a loophole. As a favour to his favourites, he'd fuck them to quench their "sinful desires." It didn't count as a sin that way, since he was part of God and everything he did was "pure" and "holy." No one thought he was behind the pregnancies. No one liked to say a bad word about him.

"Did he rape you?" I asked one of my interviewees. She scoffed and went red, part anger, part embarrassment.

"How dare you? It wasn't like that. It wasn't like that at all!"

I stayed quiet. Watched her indignation grow as the topic settled in the atmosphere. She tapped her foot, shook her thigh, fiddled with her hair. I smiled.

"Father loved us," her eyes narrowed, "and don't you forget that."

I'm glad the bastard blew his brains out when he did.

Witness #99

Three hundred and nine members. That's how many people there were in the camp and the compound combined. For me it was the entire world. Now I'm disgusted about how small-scale the whole thing was. Any time, when Camp Leader still permitted it, I could've gone into town and told someone. I didn't even consider that escape was a possibility. I thought Father was everywhere.

When I was old enough to work in the compound it seemed like he was. His voice was on a permanent tannoy. Mostly it was good news. Satisfaction and happiness rates were high in the community. The Lord said we were doing great work and that He'd see us all in the kingdom of heaven. Sometimes it was bad news. He'd tell us that "they" were coming to try and shut us down. He said that "the" wanted to kill and destroy us and take away our chance at immortality. It never occurred to me that "they" meant so many billions of people. Father taught us that you were the threat. I don't believe that anymore but lots of people do. My mother would die before she said anything against Father. I suppose you already know that if you questioned her.

When Father said he was a part of God, I pictured a tornado of colours, waves made out of souls, speaking to each of us in secret codes that only we could interpret because we were chosen and we were saved – something supernatural and beautiful that made you crumble to your knees at the sight of it. That's what I thought of when they spoke of Father. When I remembered that he was really just the man in dark glasses who delivered our food and preached at our church, I was always a little bit disappointed. The fizz of anticipation died every time when I saw him walk onto the pulpit while the crowd all screamed together. But I screamed along too.

It wasn't that we were never happy in the compound. When I saw my mother for the first time since the move, I thought my heart would explode. Her hair had grown longer and was turning grey. Tears illuminated her eyes. I don't know if she cried in happiness or horror, but she wrapped both arms around me, "my child, my child, I'm so happy to see you," her head buried into my neck. I was taller than her by then. "You're a part of The Family now. We'll be together and whole in the afterlife for all eternity." She wiped her eyes before the tears hit her cheeks and clasped my hand while she smiled. I suppose she was relieved. I'm not sure if they ever told her I was still alive. A message came over the megaphone.

"Never break vigilance. Our survival is dependent on our secrecy. They will never stop trying to destroy us." Father's voice was slurred with robotic distortion.

"Let's hope they don't get us first," I said, and my mother nodded gravely.

I know what I said then, about hoping you didn't get us. I was lying. I wanted you to come. I kept it quiet, but I always hoped that one day I might leave. I idolised you before I'd even met you, before I knew who you were or what you looked like. I still love you.

I just wish you'd found us before they took my arm.

Witness #1

#1: I found out about Mary when I cut this other girl. She was too old to be cut. She'd been here for the full five years, but for some reason they saved her till the end. Toddlers were being cut around her. She saw children come and go and join the compound while she was still in camp. Father was worried about her. He didn't think she truly believed in the word. She was always crying to be sent home and giggling through sermons. When she was eleven, I found her in town wandering around much farther out than she should've been. A brother from the compound said he saw her. Tex. He was on a secret loyalty mission from Father at the time and was posing as some sort of artist.

PO: Why do you think Father was suspicious about her?

#1: I don't really know. Maybe it was the glasses. She always seemed so sceptical. It sounds stupid to delay a cut so long because of an inkling, I know, but they kept her at the camps until she towered over the other kids, and they couldn't delay it any longer.

PO: You recognised her?

#1: Over the years you begin to know all the children, but she stuck out for me especially because she screamed so much. Usually, if that happened, you talked over them in a calming voice. That didn't stop her. She screamed in words.

PO: What did she say?

#1: She kept asking for the woman with the stars on her face. Said she was coming for her. When they bandaged her, she attempted to beat off the cutters. I'd not seen such a lack of acceptance since Johnny in the first round. He's on the compound now. He shaved his head because his fringe kept falling in his eyes while he was working. He nods when he sees me. I'm glad he bears no grudges.

PO: Keep telling me about the girl.

#1: I sat her down and tried to give her the speech, but she kept screaming. Eventually I gave up trying and asked her what woman she meant. She said she'd seen this woman in town and that she had stars tattooed onto her face. She said she was coming for her. I told her I wasn't sure what she thought she saw, and she started freaking out, kicking things around the room. Eventually I just started humouring her, asked her to describe the woman. She said she looked like a bird. Small and thin, with big eyes, and blonde hair. This woman had said she'd had a baby and was trying to escape. Apparently, this was three years ago. I knew her. That was Mary. She was the only one we'd ever known to leave the camp.

PO: You said it was impossible to leave the camp.

#1: No one really tried. Mary did, but that was it. Father said she was a sinner now. She took drugs and killed her babies with bleach and coat-hangers. He was devastated when she left. She was one of his favourites too. No amount of puri-fication could console him. When I told the girl all this, she started crying. Not like that screaming before but real tears. She tried to wipe them away, but it was awkward and clumsy. They're always so awkward and clumsy at first. Mary had said she'd come back for her. I guess when that didn't happen it broke her heart.

PO: How do you know for sure that Mary's been killed?

#1: Tattoos. She said Mary had them on her face and on her arms too, all the way up to the shoul-ders. No one else had tattoos. I let the girl go back to her mother. Her mother was good. She used to be a favourite but she's older now. I spoke to Tex afterwards. He trusted me because Father did.

He told me it'd been his job to find Mary and to hand her back to Father. She hadn't known him well enough to recognise him at the shop because cutters and fieldworkers hardly ever interacted. Tex buried the body in our cemetery where the old and the botched amputees go.

PO: I should inform you that this information will probably condemn you to life imprisonment.

#1: That's okay. I'm not exactly sure how well I'd cope with being in the real world anyway.

PO: Is there anything else you want to say?

#1: I think that's everything. Can I ask you a question though?

[A long pause.]

PO: Okay.

#1: Do you believe in paradise?

PO: No. I'm not sure. I was never raised religious.

#1: That's a shame. You know, I used to believe in it. I felt it when we sang in church, when I heard people laughing in the fields, when Father smiled at me and chose me to be cleansed. Now I don't know. I just don't know.

[The tape ends here, but not before you hear the sound of #1 sobbing.]

Epilogue:

I wrote the first edition of this book in 1995, and then decided I never wanted to hear about The Family again. I respectfully refused interviews, book-signings, and television segments. I'd told a story that wasn't mine to tell and was praised for my bravery. It wasn't until over twenty years had passed that I heard from her. She rang me on my landline number. God knows how she'd found it, or why I'd still insisted on clinging to it after all these years.

"You wrote the book about The Family atrocities, didn't you?"

Whenever I was asked that I always wanted to lie but for some reason, this time, I didn't. Some may call it divine intervention. I would not.

"You wrote about me," she said.

"I interviewed you?"

"No," she said. "You never interviewed me."

I awaited the usual flood of anger flung at me by survivors who still believed in Father's word. "Don't you realise how much he loved us?" I rubbed my temples ready for an onslaught that never came.

"I'm Witness #99."

It was a ground-floor flat in London, small and minimalist. She smoked her cigarette with her real arm, her prosthetic folded uncomfortably across her lap. She ignored the tea in front of her.

"The thing is everybody knows," she said. "Not just because of your book. They heard about it from the news. They teach it in schools now, even. People always seem to know if you're Family." She smokes, waiting for more questions.

"Why did you call me?" I asked.

"I wanted to talk to you for a while. You used a lot of my statement. It was a long statement. You thanked me in the introduction."

"You were one of the few who weren't indoctrinated."

Her eyebrows furrowed, and I wondered briefly whether she was going to laugh or cry.

"I think I was," she said. "I cried when I found out Father had died. A lot of it was anger, but some of it must've been real. And it took a while adjusting to the world." She sucked on her cigarette, looking embarrassed. I didn't press but she continued anyway. "The sex on TV… I used to start praying before I realised I didn't have to do that anymore. I think I'm okay now. The arm helps."

That was one of my proudest achievements. When the story came to light the government funded prosthetics for the children, but the sheer number was overwhelming. Half the proceeds from my book went towards helping those get private-funded healthcare. It was a huge strain on the prosthetic industry in an incredibly short period of time, but they pulled through with newer, more intelligent designs. Hers was an older, NHS model.

"I don't like my childhood," she said bluntly. "I don't like people knowing who I am. Thank you for the offer, but I'd rather people didn't see the new-fangled, robotic, intelligent design and know straight away that I'm Family." For some reason, a mental image of Witness #99 sandpapering off an Auschwitz tattoo crossed my mind. I wondered when it was exactly that I started suffering from unwanted fantasies of self-mutilation.

"I understand," I said, but I didn't really. I never saw shame in victimhood. "Do you speak to any of the other survivors?"

"No one except my mother," she said, "and I've not seen her for months. My therapist discourages me from it. My mother's still a believer, sleeps two hours a night and only eats one meal a day. "If it was good enough for Father, then it's good enough for me." A half laugh, another drag on a cigarette. "Sometimes, I think she read your book, but she wouldn't know it was me who said those things. Witness #99 could be anyone."

Her cigarette burned out, so she stumped it in the ashtray. She picked up her tea. I suddenly realised that I didn't know her name. She'd never mentioned it. It was far too late to ask now.

"You've not written a book since," she told me.

"And I don't intent to. I specialised in tragedies and exposés, but The Family was the worst I've ever seen."

"Then you're not looking hard enough." She placed down her cup, and it was quiet for a while. "Witness #1 is being released."

My stomach clenched uncomfortably as I thought about his monotone voice on the cassette tapes, laughing and crying at all the wrong moments.

"That's awful," I eventually managed. She shrugged.

"Not really. Apparently, he's a new man, completely rehabilitated. He found God, the proper one, in prison and saw the error of his ways. Now I won't keep being dragged back to testify against him every few years. It's a win/win." Her hand was shaking. I could only tell because the prosthetic was so still. "Anyway, I've moved on."

I was heading to leave and thanked her for the tea. A part of my Britishness melted away when I saw her stood there, deflated, disappointed that the interview hadn't helped her in the way she wanted. I didn't know what she expected from me, but I swallowed my pride.

"Witness #99, what's your real name?"

She laughed. "So, you do want to know? I wasn't sure."

"You knew I didn't know?"

"Of course," she said. "I never mentioned it." She reached out her hand for me to shake. "I'm Grace. Pleased to meet you."

"Well, it was lovely talking to you, Grace. I'm not entirely sure what you expect me to do with this conversation."

Grace removed her glasses to clean them, balanced them on her prosthetic hand while using the other hand to rub them with the rim of her jumper.

"Your book sells constantly. Just slam it in the epilogue for the next edition."

"Okay." I smiled. "I think I'll be able to do that."

She carefully placed her glasses back on her face.

"Much better," she said. "Yes, this is much better now."

English to American Dictionary

As pointed out by my very lovely but very American publishers, my work can be alienating for those who aren't used to my specific brand of northern English dialect. Therefore, I thought it might be helpful to leave you with this dictionary.

Biro: The most boring pen brand usually bought in bulk and found in offices and schools. (Please don't sue me, Biro. We all have subjective feelings about stationary.)

Bob: Old money, a.k.a. a shilling.

A cheeky, bloody article: Someone who's rude or bold, but also quite likeable and funny.

Diddy: Short.

Dimp: The filter end of a cigarette, (the butt).

"Don't know you're born": To be unaware of how privileged or lucky you are, particularly in comparison to others.

Ginnel: The alleyway between two houses.

Het up: to get excited or upset.

Int: Short for "isn't."

Nowt: Short for "nothing."'

OAPs: Old-Aged Pensioners.

Owt: Short for "anything."

Sweeties: Candy.

Tannoy: British manufacturer of loudspeakers. Tannoy announcements are heard in shops, train stations, and occasionally the agricultural areas of Jonestown-esque cults.

Wee: Pee.

"Went spare": to get angry or upset.

Book Club Questions

1) What do these stories say about human nature?

2) In what ways do these stories reflect the real world as you perceive it?

3) Which story in this collection is the most impactful for you right now? Why do you think that is? What do you think you would have said five years ago? Ten years ago?

4) Many of these stories deal with domestic abuse spanning centuries—what does this say about our society? Has the position of women improved at all?

5) Some of these stories utilise first-person perspective to pull the reader into the narrative. How did you feel reading these inner thoughts, specifically in "Proud Boy, and "Hands Up"?

6) "Centurion" focuses on the anger of an old woman—what does her perspective on her life say about the way society treats the elderly?

7) "Your Son's Good at Times Tables" showcases a familiar situation—someone wants to speak up but doesn't and then obsesses about what should have been said--can you relate to this feeling of missing the moment to connect?

8) What do you think the image of fire symbolises in "Pitchforks and Vicodin" and "The Original Story of Kerosene Girl"? Do you think it works effectively?

9) "The Old Castle" shows the conflict between assimilation and equality, and the maintaining of queer culture. Who do you agree with? Roxanne or the narrator? Why do you think so?

10) Many of these stories: "White Butterflies," "Blank Face," and "Oh, Rats!" deal with grief and survivor's guilt. What do you think the author is trying to say about grief? Do you feel this is an accurate representation of suffering?

C. D.

Author Bio

Cathleen Davies is a writer, teacher, and researcher from East Yorkshire, England. Her work has appeared in a number of magazines and anthologies. She likes live music, cheap lager, and long walks on the beach. This is her first solo collection.

www.ingramcontent.com/pod-product-compliance
Lightning Source LLC
Chambersburg PA
CBHW020420110726
47899CB00006B/2070